LOVE GAME

Rowena Winston had enjoyed working with her dear friend Donald. Together they had turned Chalford Manor into an excellent hotel and country club. But now Donald was dead, and she had the far greater challenge of working with his younger brother Clive — a man who had every reason to resent her!

*Books by Diney Delancey
in the Linford Romance Library:*

FOR LOVE OF OLIVER
AN OLD-FASHIONED LOVE
LOVE'S DAWNING
SILVERSTRAND
BRAVE HEART
THE SLOPES OF LOVE
THE SECRET OF SHEARWATER
KISS AND TELL
A CHANCE OF HAPPINESS

DINEY DELANCEY

LOVE GAME

Complete and Unabridged

LINFORD
Leicester

First published in Great Britain in 1986

First Linford Edition
published 2007

British Library CIP Data

DeLancey, Diney
   Love game.—Large print ed.—
   Linford romance library
   1. Country clubs—Fiction
   2. Love stories
   3. Large type books
   I. Title
   823.9′14 [F]

   ISBN 978–1–84782–033–4

Published by
F. A. Thorpe (Publishing)
Anstey, Leicestershire

Set by Words & Graphics Ltd.
Anstey, Leicestershire
Printed and bound in Great Britain by
T. J. International Ltd., Padstow, Cornwall

This book is printed on acid-free paper

1

Rowena Winston was sitting waiting for David Kelland, Donald's solicitor. She stared across the formal gardens laid out in front of Chalford Manor, to the avenue which led to the gates, and wondered why he had asked to see her. The limes which edged the avenue stood motionless in the sunshine with no breath of wind to stir their leaves. The sky arched blue and cloudless above and Rowena could smell the scent of the early roses growing below her open window.

It was the first fine day there had been since Donald had died. Even at the funeral yesterday the sky had been cold and grey, with scudding clouds and flurries of rain. Now, almost imperceptibly as she prepared to try and resume her life, Rowena felt her spirits lift.

The gleam of sunshine on a windscreen drew her attention to a car coming up the avenue. As it turned on to the smooth gravel in front of the house, Rowena glanced at her watch. Mr. Kelland had arrived punctually for his appointment, and seeing him get out of his car Rowena went down to the front hall to meet him.

'Miss Winston, good morning,' David Kelland greeted her cheerfully, his hand extended.

'Nicc to see you, Mr. Kelland. Will you come up to my office? We can talk privately there.' She turned to Gilly, the receptionist, and added, 'Have some coffee sent up to us please, Gilly.'

Once they were settled in Rowena's office with the coffee before them, the solicitor came straight to the point.

'I'm sorry to have to come to see you so soon after Donald's death,' he said. 'If it were merely business, I'd have left it a couple of weeks — until you were more on your feet, so to speak.'

Rowena smiled at him, maintaining

her calm exterior. 'Don't worry, Mr. Kelland. I'm back on my feet. Donald's death was a tremendous shock, of course, but I find keeping busy is the best treatment of all. There's always so much to do here, that I haven't had time to think.'

David Kelland returned her smile. He liked Rowena Winston. She was a determined woman, resourceful, and he had watched her help Donald Latimer turn Chalford Manor into a really first-class hotel and country club. It was the knowledge that their success was largely due to Rowena that made the purpose of this visit so much more difficult. He glanced across at her admiringly, taking in the smooth dark hair which today she wore drawn back from her face and tied with a green scarf at the nape of her neck, her dark eyes, wide and candid, and the smile still hovering on her lips as she waited for him to speak. She was, as always, an extremely attractive woman.

'The trouble is,' he said reluctantly,

bringing his mind back to the business he had come to discuss, 'we haven't got Donald's Will. We've a copy of course, but the original was sent to him at his request for signature, and he never returned it to us.'

'He certainly received it,' said Rowena. 'He told me what was in it and I thought he was joking so he showed it to me. He left everything to me.'

★ ★ ★

David Kelland nodded. 'I know,' he agreed. 'I drew it up, but I don't have the signed original. The only signed Will of Donald's I have is the previous one, where he left everything to his brother Clive. You haven't heard from *him*, I suppose?'

Rowena shook her head.

'No. I wrote to him, of course, at the address in Donald's address book, but I've had no reply. I thought he'd come to the funeral yesterday but there was no sign of him. I know they weren't on

4

good terms — Donald said they hadn't really spoken to each other for years. Even so, you'd have thought he'd have made the effort to come to his own brother's funeral, wouldn't you?'

'You would,' agreed David Kelland. 'But perhaps he's away or something and hasn't got your letter yet. Did you try ringing?'

'Of course. But Donald had no number listed, and when I tried directory enquiries they said it was ex-directory and they weren't allowed to give it.'

The solicitor shrugged. 'Well, you may still hear from him — after all it's only a week. But even so you really must go through Donald's papers as soon as possible and find the new Will so that we can get on and get probate granted as quickly as we can.'

Rowena frowned slightly and said, 'Of course. You shall have it as soon as I find it, but with Donald's death being so sudden everything is at sixes and sevens. I've the hotel and the club to run as well as the business of sorting out Donald's things . . . '

She broke off and David Kelland said awkwardly, 'I know. It won't be easy for a while yet, but keeping the business going will help you through this difficult time, you know. We'll help in every possible way, both with the routine things — like getting the licence put into your name — and with the terms of the Will once you've found the one Donald signed.' The solicitor rose to his feet. Setting his empty coffee cup aside, he went on, 'Just let me know what I can do to help. I'm here if you need me.'

After David Kelland had gone, Rowena returned to her desk. She sat staring out across the gardens again and thought about Donald and Chalford. Donald Latimer had taken over Chalford Golf Club, an ailing concern whose membership had dwindled alarmingly. Determined to infuse it with new life, he had also bought the deserted Georgian manor house in whose grounds the golf course was laid out. By renovating the manor and converting it into an hotel, and extending the golf club facilities so that tennis and riding were also available, he was able to advertise the premises as a country club and hotel and thus appeal to a far wider clientèle.

It was after the first complete season, when Donald had been able to see that his imaginative investment was going to pay off, that Rowena joined his staff. She had been at Chalford Manor now for five years, first as receptionist-cum-secretary working directly for Donald, and then, as the hotel and country club really got off the ground, becoming more and more involved with the actual planning and running of the place.

Increasingly, Donald came to rely on her as she helped him develop new ideas and oversaw the day-to-day running of the club. The days when she would spend her time behind the reception desk dealing with members and guests, or hammering at her typewriter, were long gone. Gilly did all that very ably now, under Rowena's supervision, and she herself took overall responsibility for the whole set up, overseeing everything from the running of the kitchen to the régime in the stables. Donald, delighted with her aptitude, had encouraged her to become more and more involved.

Then one day he had asked Rowena to marry him.

'There's no need to give me a quick answer,' he had said. 'Take your time — I can wait. Just remember I love you, and will do, whatever your answer.'

⋆　⋆　⋆

Rowena had given his proposal of marriage serious thought. It offered her comfort and security, companionship and affection — but eventually, after much heart-searching, she had decided against it. Such a marriage would not be for love, and though she knew Donald loved her in his way she would have felt dishonest accepting his offer without being able to offer much in return.

In her own mind Rowena was sure she would never marry, even though she knew men found her attractive and she enjoyed their company. What she did not enjoy was actual physical contact.

That distaste went back a long way, to an unfortunate incident when she had been up at university. A casual boy friend whom she had invited in to coffee had misconstrued the invitation. Occasionally the memory of his hands on her body, his unwelcome mouth upon hers, would catch her unawares and make cold sweat break on her forehead. Any sign of a man wanting physical intimacy, even if only a kiss and caress, she saw as a threat and always tried to forestall such an overture.

Strangely, Donald had not posed this sort of threat until he actually asked her to marry him. With their easy friendship well-established, Rowena was reluctant to let things develop further, afraid she might hurt him in her rejection of his inevitable love-making. It was not the sort of partnership she wanted, and so gently, and with some regret, she turned him down. He had accepted her refusal philosophically and insisted that it made no difference to her place at Chalford Manor. Everything would go on as before.

Then, last year, he'd brought home his Will and shown it to her.

'There!' he said proudly. 'I've left it all to you, Ro. You've made this place what it is, built up its reputation in a very short time. So when I die, it'll be yours.' She stared at him, astonished, and he looked at her anxiously. They were in his sitting-room in the garden wing, having a quiet drink before the evening guests arrived in the restaurant. In the incredulous silence which had greeted his announcement, he said, 'You are pleased, aren't you? Just because you won't marry me doesn't mean you haven't earned this, you know.'

Rowena smiled back at him.

'Of course I'm pleased. I'm stunned! It really is very generous of you, and you know I love every stick and stone of the place. It's just that I'd never dreamt . . . I mean . . .'

'Good,' said Donald. 'That's settled. Then we'll drink to the future owner of Chalford Manor. Cheers.'

Rowena obediently raised her glass. 'Cheers,' she said, 'but don't forget the future owner won't be taking over for years yet.'

'No,' agreed Donald. 'Let's hope not. But all eventualities are covered now and none of our work will be wasted. Everything would be safely in your hands and go on as smoothly as ever.'

He must have known his heart was suspect, Rowena decided as she gave considered thought to Donald's Will for the first time since his heart attack the week before. He had certainly drawn away from the routine running of the club and hotel, increasingly leaving things to her, but until now she had not realised quite how much and had not ascribed this to his health. He must have known he could die at any time and that was why he had made his Will and shown it to her. Dear Donald. How brave he had been, shouldering the knowledge of his death sentence alone.

'Nothing'll change, Donald, I promise,' said Rowena aloud to her empty office. 'I'll run the place as if you were still here.'

With this resolve, she set herself to the task she had been avoiding for days, entering Donald's private office and beginning to clear his desk. She had been to the desk several times since his heart attack had struck so unexpectedly and mercilessly, but only to seek details concerning the day-to-day running of Chalford Manor Country Club; she had not been systematically through the files or the drawers of the desk. With some reluctance she settled to this task

now, sorting his papers into piles, each
to be dealt with at a later date.

★   ★   ★

Of course she was keeping an eye out
for the Will as she went, but strangely
enough it was not uppermost in her
mind as she sorted through the letters
and papers she found. She wondered if
she would discover any more about his
family. He had seldom mentioned
anyone but his mother and though
Rowena had known of his brother
Clive's existence, that was all she did
know of him. She found nothing further
in Donald's desk.

She concentrated on the personal
files, feeling that he was more likely to
have placed his Will amongst these
papers than the business ones in the
steel cabinet. As she glanced at the
letters in his private correspondence
files, Rowena discovered there was
much about Donald she had not
known. One box contained letters from

children in India whom Donald had been sponsoring through a charity. There were three children, a boy and two girls, and from their case histories which were enclosed in the same box it was clear that Donald's involvement went back ten years or more. Yet Rowena had had no inkling of it during his life.

There was another box crammed full of photographs, many in black and white, yellowing with age. In some a much younger Donald was clearly visible, his hair darker then, without the silver frosting Rowena always associated with him. He had the same deep-set eyes and jutting, clefted chin, the same attractive smile creased his face with pleasure, and Rowena realised with a jolt what a really handsome man he had once been. By the time she had known him he was past fifty and his startling good looks had lost their youthful edge. Although he still retained the attractiveness of the young man in the photographs, his expression had become gentler; no, not gentler exactly, Rowena thought as she studied the faded prints, but less uncompromising, the face of a man who had come to terms with the world and himself.

With a sigh, she set the box aside and continued her search. By lunchtime she had found nothing significant. A weary afternoon at the filing cabinet yielded nothing either until Rowena found a piece of paper with a sequence of numbers on it at the back of a drawer. Suddenly she remembered the small wall safe Donald had in his own flat in the garden wing.

'Of course,' she said aloud. 'How stupid of me to have forgotten the safe! That's where it'll be.' She let herself out of the house and, clutching the piece of paper, crossed the garden to Donald's flat.

Unlocking the door, she paused for a moment on the threshold, allowing the warm and sunny silence of the familiar living-room to wash over her. She had avoided Donald's flat up until now, fearing to find it cold and empty.

But it was not cold. The sun had warmed it as always in the afternoons, and the peaceful comfort of the room was undisturbed rather than empty, almost as if Donald might return at any moment. Rowena felt the tears prick her eyes as she realised yet again how much she would miss him, how strong their friendship had been. But she blinked back her tears and with new determination stepped across the room and lifted a picture from the wall, revealing the safe behind it.

Using the combination she had found in the filing cabinet, she opened its door. There, beside a cash box and a jewel case, lay the Will, rolled and tied with a piece of dull pink tape. Rowena lifted it out and glanced at the opening lines.

Yes, this was it, the Will Donald had shown her just a year ago. She carried it over to one of the deep armchairs, warm in a shaft of afternoon sun, and sank down to read it again. But she sat up with a jolt as she glanced at the bottom to see its date. For a moment she stared down at the document in her hand and then she got up and crossed hurriedly to the phone.

'David Kelland, please.'

She was put through quickly and on hearing David Kelland's voice said, 'David? I've found it. Donald's Will.'

'Rowena! That's great,' he began.

'No, it isn't,' she cried. 'He didn't sign it. Donald didn't sign the Will.'

★   ★   ★

There was silence for a moment and then the solicitor said in a careful tone, 'I see.' He paused again, then, 'You are sure it's the original, Rowena, aren't you?'

'Quite sure.'

'Hmm. This is rather serious news. Why don't you come in and see me — bring the Will with you.'

Rowena drew a long breath. 'No,' she said flatly. 'Not straight away, anyway.

17

Just tell me the worst.'

'I'm afraid it's horrifyingly simple,' David Kelland said. 'Although we know Donald intended to alter his Will, and actually drew up the new one, unless the second is signed and witnessed the previous Will still stands and we have to execute that.'

'And that says?'

'It says he leaves everything to his brother, Clive. He made it before you came to Chalford Manor, so of course you're not mentioned.'

'I see.' Rowena's voice was bleak. 'So what happens now?'

'We shall have to contact Clive Latimer. He may or may not know that he was his brother's sole beneficiary. Donald may even have told him that he'd altered his Will in your favour.'

'Any chance of contesting it?'

'Not really,' the solicitor said regretfully. 'If you'd been his widow we might have got somewhere. Believe me, Rowena, I'm very sorry this has happened. When we sent the Will for signature we offered to put it into safe keeping, but Donald said no. He said he'd keep the original himself, and we should keep the copy.'

'And his previous Will wasn't destroyed?'

'No. We never destroy a signed Will unless we have the next to supersede it.'

'But you had the next one.'

'Only a copy. Not the original.'

There was an awkward silence. To break it, David Kelland said, 'As Donald's named executors we must formally ask you to keep Chalford ticking over until we hear from Mr. Latimer as to what he's going to do with the place. After all, he may want you to continue running things as before.'

'Rubbish,' Rowena screamed silently. 'Nothing will ever be the same again.' Aloud she said abruptly; 'You'd better let me know what he says, then. I'll wait for your call. Goodbye.'

And before the solicitor could say any more, Rowena cut off the call. She replaced the receiver and crossed back to the armchair. Sunlight still flooded the room, dancing on the deep blues and greens of the carpet, but Rowena felt cold and to her the room looked grey and colourless.

★ ★ ★

Rowena passed the next two weeks in a daze. The day after she found Donald's Will, she decided she should talk to David Kelland after all and went to his office. He confirmed that they would have to execute the earlier Will, and made a formal request for her to keep Chalford Manor going until his firm had managed to contact Clive Latimer. Rowena agreed and, returning to Chalford, continued to see to the smooth running of the hotel and country club. The normal programme of events was maintained, and the staff, as always, came and consulted her when there were any problems.

The staff was a fairly large one,

including indoor staff, a golf professional and a riding instructress. Each
was well able to continue in the normal
way, but there was a section of the
country club which was a compartively
new venture and she watched over that
carefully.

One of Donald's few recent innovations had been the retaining of a
full-time tennis coach, Barry Short, for
the summer months. Children's classes
had been organised for Saturday
mornings and were well attended, and
many of the lady members had begun
to take private lessons from him — not
always, Rowena thought a little cyni-
cally, to better their performance on
the tennis court. Barry Short was a
very good player and a competent
coach. He was also an extremely
attractive man with a thick shock of
curling dark hair and wide brown eyes.
The smile which lurked permanently
around his full sensual lips would
broaden appreciatively as he surveyed
the women who frequented the club,

and in particular those who came to him for coaching. His over easy charm sometimes gave Rowena cause for anxiety.

Donald had allocated him a small cottage at the edge of the golf course and Barry seldom actually came into the country club, except on routine matters or for a drink in the bar. So Rowena was surprised when one evening she glanced up and found him propped against her office doorway, watching her working at her desk.

'Hello, Barry,' she said. 'Problems?'

He smiled and shook his head. 'No,' he replied. 'I just thought you might fancy a game of tennis. It's a lovely evening and only two of the courts are in use.'

Rowena shook her head. 'It's a nice thought,' she said with a smile, 'but I haven't finished here yet.'

'Leave it,' said Barry firmly. 'Come on, it'll do you good to get out of here. I'll wait in the bar while you change.'

Rowena opened her mouth to protest

but Barry pointed to the door and said severely, 'Out! Upstairs and change.'

Suddenly, she felt he was right. She did need to get out of the office, and the exercise would do her good.

'All right,' she said, 'I won't be long,' and went up to her flat under the eaves to get ready.

★   ★   ★

Rowena enjoyed the game with Barry, and on several evenings after that he came and rooted her out of the office to play a set or two before it got dark. Until then Rowena had hardly known him, but now she found him extremely good company. She was well aware of the effect his easy charm was having on some of the lady members but when she found he did not attempt to make a pass at her, as she had half-suspected he might, she relaxed and a comfortable friendship developed quickly between them. Rowena was extremely grateful for it. She missed Donald far more than she would have dreamed possible; not in the actual managing of the club and hotel, she had been doing that almost unaided for some time, but in the little things. She missed having someone to talk to, and Barry's friendship compensated her a little. After their tennis they would usually have a shandy on the terrace, chatting comfortably.

Of course Rowena did not mention Donald's Will or the expectations she had had of it, but there was great speculation among the staff as to what would happen when Mr. Clive Latimer finally turned up.

'If it were me,' Barry told her frankly one evening, 'I'd be delighted to let everything go on as before. I'd certainly keep everyone on, and you in particular.'

'I'm not sure I really want to stay,' Rowena admitted. 'There are too many memories for me here. I think perhaps I need a complete change.'

'Were you in love with Donald Latimer?'

Rowena was startled at the unexpected question. 'I beg your pardon?'

'Were you in love with Donald Latimer?'

'No, as a matter of fact I wasn't — if it's any business of yours.'

'It isn't,' said Barry with a smile. 'I shouldn't have asked. I'm sorry.'

Rowena sighed. 'It's all right. It doesn't matter. I wasn't in love with him, but I loved him dearly as a friend, corny as that may sound.'

A silence fell between them for a moment and then Barry said, 'Tennis tomorrow evening?'

Rowena shook her head. 'No, I'm afraid not. There's golfing society coming tomorrow, and I'll be busy with them — they play two rounds of golf and then there's a reception and dinner in the evening.'

'Sounds like a long day.'

'I think it will be,' admitted Rowena, and got to her feet. 'So I must go and check everything's all right in the restaurant this evening, and then I think

I'll have an early night.'

The first members of the golfing society were due to play off at 8.30 a.m., and they began arriving a little before that. Rowena was at the door to greet their secretary, and for a while the reception was extremely busy, many of the golfers having booked into the hotel so that they would not have to drive home after the dinner in the evening. But at last the rush was over and Rowena escaped to her office with a cup of coffee, leaving Gilly to cope single-handed at the desk.

For a moment she stood at the window, drinking her coffee, and as she did so, saw the arrival of another car up the lime avenue. 'Well, the rush is over,' she thought. 'Most of the golfers are already out on the course, and Gilly can cope with this late arrival.' She turned reluctantly to the paperwork which had accumulated on her desk.

After a moment or two's concentrated work she was aware of the bell at reception being rung loud and long. As it rang again, Rowena realised Gilly couldn't be there and went down to answer it.

A man was waiting, his fingers drumming impatiently on the desk top as he gazed round the entrance hall. He stood with his back to the sunlight which flooded in through the open front door and for a moment Rowena saw him only in silhouette.

She came down the wide flight of stairs with a welcoming smile.

'Good morning, sir, can I help you?'

'Is the desk usually left unmanned?' the man asked abruptly.

'Not usually,' she replied tightly. 'I'm sure Gilly can't be far away. She must have stepped out for a moment. Can I help you? I'm Rowena Winston — I run this hotel.' She moved behind the reception desk and the visitor turned towards her. The light fell across his face. She drew in a sharp breath and hardly heard him as he said: 'My name's Clive Latimer, and I own this hotel.'

* * *

It could have been Donald standing in front of her, or at least the younger Donald of the photographs she had found. The eyes, the chin and the firm mouth were just the same, only the expression was wrong. Where Donald had mellowed, looking out at the world with amusement and understanding in his eyes, Clive Latimer seemed harsh and uncompromising. His face held no laughter and he frowned at Rowena as she stared across the desk at him.

'Is there something wrong with my appearance, Miss Winston?' he asked mildly.

She felt herself colour as she had not done in years and said huskily, 'No of course not. It's just that . . . ' She broke off, embarrassed.

'Just what?' he prompted.

'You look so like Donald.'

Clive gave a grim smile. 'Do I? How unfortunate. Now perhaps,' he went on smoothly, 'you could call your receptionist to take over and then we could go somewhere private to talk.'

'Yes, of course,' she said. 'I'll just find her.' As she spoke, Gilly appeared through the front door looking flushed. Angry that Clive Latimer should have found them with the reception desk unattended, Rowena said sharply: 'Where've you been, Gilly? You shouldn't have left the desk on such a busy morning.'

'I'm sorry,' the girl replied, 'only Mrs. Morton-Harvey phoned to cancel her tennis with Barry and I went out to tell him. He wasn't at the courts so I had to go over to the cottage, but he wasn't . . . '

'I see,' Rowena cut in. 'Well, another time let me know and I'll keep an eye on the desk for you.' She came round the counter and said to Clive, 'If you'll come this way, Mr. Latimer, we'll go into my office.'

She led the way briskly across the hall. Glancing back, she noticed that though Clive Latimer was following her, he walked slowly with a heavy limp and had to use a walking stick. Perhaps she should suggest that they use the lift instead of the flight of stairs? One look at the man's face decided her to say nothing. She merely walked a little more slowly herself and led him into her office.

'So, Miss Winston, it sounds from what David Kelland says in his letter we have a good deal to discuss.'

He did not seat himself in the chair Rowena indicated but limped across to the window and looked out across the formal garden. She closed the door behind them so that their discussion should not be overheard and then walked over to her desk, intending to seat herself behind it as if by putting it between them she would be safe from the aura of disdain which emanated from the man at the window.

But as she passed near him he suddenly swung round to face her and his hand snaked out to grab her wrist and jerk her into his arms. He silenced the yelp of surprise she gave by covering her mouth with his own in a violent kiss. The blood thundered in her ears as a cold wave of panic engulfed her but even as Rowena fought to break free of him, to twist her face away from his, she knew the struggle was hopeless. She was clamped in the steel grip of his arms which only tightened as she tried in vain to wrench herself free. At length she ceased struggling. As he felt her give up the fight, Clive suddenly released her, pushing her abruptly aside with an expression of disgust on his face.

★　★　★

Rowena staggered as he thrust her from him. Clutching her desk for support, she felt her sickening panic subside as he said contemptuously, 'Was that the sort of thing you had in mind? Hadn't you planned for us to become as intimately acquainted as you and Donald were? Don't tell me I moved too fast for you, Miss Winston. Surely you're not a girl to let the grass grow under your feet?'

'How dare you?' hissed Rowena as she gathered her breath. 'How dare you touch me?'

'Come, come, my *dear* Miss Winston,' Clive said, mildly chiding. 'Isn't that how you managed to persuade my dear foolish brother to re-make his Will, by the use of your delectable body?'

Rowena stared at him incredulously.

'So,' he went on, 'you managed to persuade Donald to make a new Will but forgot to get him to sign it. Careless.'

Already ice-cold with fury, she felt the colour drain from her cheeks as the significance of his words hit home. She gripped the edge of her desk fiercely with her hands, and it was only this that stopped her from hitting out at the man watching her, wiping that smile of contempt from his face. How dare he cast such a slur on her, or on Donald either? White with controlled rage she said softly and distinctly: 'Donald made that Will by his own choice. I had no part of it. It was his idea to leave this place to me.'

Clive Latimer seemed amused at her anger. 'A pity for you that he forgot to sign it then — or perhaps he changed his mind,' he said lightly. 'So careless of you not to check.'

'He did not change his mind as far as I know,' Rowena snapped.

'He must have,' asserted Clive. 'After all, though the Will was drawn up a year ago, it wasn't signed.'

She could find no further answers, merely sat down shakily while Clive Latimer, satisfied that for the moment he had had the best of the argument, crossed to a chair and sat down to face her.

'When exactly did Donald die?' he began casually, but it was too much. Rowena got to her feet, shaking with fury at his casual enquiry.

'He died three weeks ago and you've taken until now to come and find out about him. I wrote to you the evening he died, to tell you. You didn't even come to the funeral! As far as I know you're his only living relative and yet you couldn't even make the effort to come to his funeral. The solicitors have written to you and you haven't even bothered to answer their letters. You — you're contemptible! You come here implying that I've tricked Donald into leaving me his business — Donald, one of my dearest friends. How dare you? It's you who's wrong.

'Donald *did* mean me to have the hotel — he was pleased not to have to leave it to you. Pleased! He didn't want anything to do with you. You haven't earned Chalford Manor, but I have. I've helped him to turn it into a going concern; he wanted it to continue the way it was going and that's why he left it to me. Even in the new circumstances I might have continued to work here, perhaps, so that what he wanted would have been carried out despite the Will's being wrong. But as it is . . . '

She was interrupted by a loud knock

on the door which heralded Gilly's appearance.

'Rowena, I'm sorry to trouble you — ' she began.

'What is it?' snapped Rowena. 'What do you want?'

'Mr. Harland from room 18 says that his wallet has been stolen from his room.' Gilly looked at Rowena anxiously. 'Could you come down a minute?'

She took a deep breath and forced herself to smile. 'Yes, of course. Mr. Latimer and I have finished our discussion.'

She followed Gilly to the door and then, looking back towards Clive Latimer who was still sitting watching her, Rowena said quietly, 'My month's notice starts from this minute. If you find someone to replace me sooner, so much the better.'

2

Rowena went down to reception and, forcing a smile to her face, went over to Mr. Harland.

'I demand that the police are sent for at once,' he said before she could speak. 'My wallet has gone from my room and it had nearly a hundred pounds in it, and my credit cards.'

'Of course, Mr. Harland,' Rowena answered smoothly. 'I'll phone them in just one moment, but I'd like to check the safe first. Occasionally lost valuables are handed in and it is just possible the night porter may have been given your wallet and forgotten to mention that he'd put it into the safe before he went off duty.'

Mr. Harland opened his mouth to protest but Rowena went on, 'I won't keep you one moment, sir,' and went into the back office to the safe which housed guests' valuables. When she returned empty-handed she found Clive Latimer also at the reception desk, but she ignored him and turned once more to Mr. Harland.

'I'm afraid your wallet hasn't been handed in, sir, so if I could just take a few particulars I'll phone the police for you.'

She wrote down a description of the man's wallet noting its contents and where it had been hidden in the room.

'I slipped it under the mattress while I went out to hit a few balls on the practice ground,' Harland complained, 'and when I came back it had gone. It must have been the chamber maid when she made the bed.'

Rowena was angry at the unfounded accusation, and said tightly, 'I doubt that, sir. Amy has been with us for some time and we've never had cause to question her honesty. It is a great pity, if I may say so, that you did not hand in your wallet for safe-keeping at the desk. The hotel takes no responsibility for valuables left unattended in guests' rooms.'

'It was only for an hour,' the man snapped angrily.

'Even so, sir,' said Rowena. 'Now, if you'd care to wait in the lounge, Gilly will bring you some coffee and I will call the police.'

Still muttering angrily, Mr. Harland went into the lounge and Rowena dialled the local police station.

All the time she had been dealing with the theft, she had been conscious of Clive Latimer at her elbow, and his obvious appraisal of her handling of the situation. Shaken by this, and angry at his witnessing the unfortunate affair at all, she found that her hands were shaking as she replaced the receiver after her call.

★ ★ ★

As she was still standing at the desk she turned to him at last and said icily, 'Yes, Mr. Latimer?'

'I'm going to see Kelland now,' he said, 'but I shall be back later. At some stage I shall want to go over the accounts, look at the bookings and the details of the facilities we offer. I should also like to meet the staff, so that they know who they work for now.'

'I'm afraid that won't be very convenient today,' said Rowena. 'We've a large golfing society here for whom we're doing a running buffet at lunchtime, and a reception and dinner this evening.'

'And the police will be carrying on their enquiries amongst them all,' Clive Latimer added.

'They'll be very discreet, they always are.' Even as she spoke Rowena could have bitten her tongue, and Clive Latimer certainly did not miss the slip she had made.

'You mean they've had to be called in before?'

'Occasionally, yes.' Rowena tried to sound casual. 'In a hotel and country club this size, it's inevitable that occasionally things go missing; there are members and guests, as well as the odd member of staff, who aren't above a bit of petty pilfering.'

'I see,' he said. 'It's another thing we'll have to discuss later. But in view of your programme for today we'll leave our meeting until tomorrow. Perhaps you'd set aside some time for it then. I will be back later, however.'

'Would you like a room prepared for you in the hotel?' Rowena asked reluctantly. She had no wish for Clive Latimer to be on hand to watch her every move. He had already caught them out in inefficiency and seen the unfortunate episode regarding the missing wallet; she felt sure he was just waiting to catch them out further. But his answer upset her even more than the fact he would be there to check up on her.

'No, thank you,' he replied smoothly. 'I'll move into my brother's flat. Perhaps you'd be good enough to move out of it and to have it cleaned while I'm out.'

He stepped away but stopped abruptly when Rowena, ice cold with rage, hissed after him, 'Mr. Latimer.'

He turned back casually, his dark eyes mocking her, and added: 'If that will be convenient, Miss Winston.'

'I do not live in your brother's flat, nor have I ever done so. I have my own rooms at the top of the hotel.'

Apparently unperturbed by the blazing fury in her eyes, Clive Latimer nodded.

'Good,' he said lightly. 'Then preparing the flat for me to use will be no problem. Good morning, Miss Winston.' And before Rowena could gather her wits to answer him, he turned abruptly away and limped out to the car that awaited him in the drive. Through the hotel's open doors, Rowena saw a driver get out and assist him into the passenger seat.

The relief of seeing him go was enormous, but even so the damp mist of depression and foreboding which had descended on her at his appearance did not lift. She was angry with his assumption that she'd tricked Donald into leaving Chalford to her, angry with herself for her incompetent handling of his insinuations, and angry that nothing he had seen so far put the hotel into a good light.

★   ★   ★

Gilly had returned from ordering Mr. Harland's coffee. Rowena turned to her and said, 'You did tell Barry about Mrs. Morton-Harvey?'

'No, I didn't,' the girl said. 'I couldn't find him. Shall I go out to the courts again now?'

'No, I'll go,' said Rowena. 'I need a breath of fresh air. I'll only be five minutes and then I'll check with Danny in the kitchen. It won't be long before the first golfers are in for lunch.'

'There's no problem there. It's all laid out ready in the dining-room — I saw it when I asked Gwen to do Mr. Harland's coffee.'

'Fine, I shan't be long.'

She stepped out into the May sunshine and drew in a deep breath of sweet summer air. For a moment she stood there, letting the warmth of the sun vanquish the chill she still felt after her encounter with Clive Latimer. Then she strolled across to the tennis courts.

No one was playing but she heard voices in the little pavilion to one side of court one and went across to speak to Barry. The door was ajar. As Rowena approached, the voices died away. To her surprise she saw that Barry was indeed in the pavilion and so, clasped in a passionate embrace with him, was Beryl, one of the waitresses from the hotel. Too engrossed in their kiss to hear Rowena's entrance, they both jumped guiltily apart when she cried sharply: 'Beryl! Barry! What do you think you're doing?'

★ ★ ★

Beryl blushed crimson and hastily adjusted her disarrayed clothing, but Barry looked across at Rowena and grinned. 'Nothing very drastic, I do assure you,' he drawled. 'Beryl was just bringing me a cup of coffee.'

'Go back indoors, Beryl,' Rowena said abruptly. 'The early golfers'll be in for lunch before long, and I'm sure Danny needs you.'

Still blushing furiously, Beryl made good her escape while Rowena turned on Barry.

'How could you? We've enough trouble without your seducing the waitresses.'

He continued to smile. 'I'm not sure I was doing the seducing,' he said.

'I don't care who started it,' said Rowena crossly. 'Just behave yourself.'

She gave him the message about Mrs. Morton-Harvey and then told him briefly that Clive Latimer had been and was coming back later.

'He wants to meet all the staff,' she said, 'and we'd all better watch our step.'

'Point taken,' he said mischievously. 'I'll be good. What's he like anyway, this Clive Latimer?'

She took a deep breath. 'Pompous, arrogant, self-opinionated, rude, over-bearing — '

Barry guffawed. 'Steady on,' he cried, 'something tells me our new boss hasn't made a hit with you.'

'He hasn't. But it doesn't matter, because my notice is in and I'm out as soon as possible.'

Barry pulled a face. 'Never mind,' he consoled her, 'you can always come back as a member and pay him no attention at all.'

Rowena laughed unwillingly. 'No thanks,' she said. 'I can't shake the dust of this place off my feet soon enough.'

Footsteps sounded outside and Rowena glanced out to see Angela Thomas approaching the court.

'Here's your next lesson,' she said. 'I'll see you later.'

Returning to the hotel, she thanked heaven that she had not had Clive with her when she'd discovered Barry and Beryl in the pavilion. She could just imagine his contemptuous reaction. It made her cold to think of it.

⋆　⋆　⋆

As she reached the front door a police car drew up in the drive beside her. She knew the officers inside, Sergeant Doller and Constable Prout. They walked in with her and she introduced them to Mr. Harland, and then lent them her office to talk privately.

'We'd like a word with you too, Miss Winston, before we go.'

'Of course,' she agreed. 'I'll be in the dining-room, I expect. Just ask Gilly to give me a call.'

While she cast an appraising eye over the cold table laid out there, Rowena thought about Mr. Harland and his wallet.

'It's his own fault for leaving it under the mattress,' she decided. 'Of all the stupid places to hide money and credit cards.'

But she was really very worried. As she had let slip in front of Clive Latimer, this was not the first time valuables had disappeared. Despite what she had said to him, there had been very little pilfering at Chalford in the past; it was only comparatively recently that it had been on the increase. Money had disappeared from the changing rooms, and one or two of the hotel guests had lost money and trinkets from their rooms . . .

'Is there something wrong with that table?' demanded a voice behind her. She turned to find Danny, the chef, standing watching her. 'Only you've been standing staring at it for a good five minutes,' he said.

Rowena laughed. 'Sorry, Danny,' she said. 'I was miles away.'

'I hear Clive Latimer was here this morning,' he said. 'Could he be the cause of your trouble?'

'Partly, I suppose,' she admitted. 'I

wasn't expecting him — and today of all days.'

'Well, he can't have any complaints about that. He must be delighted to see the business we're doing. I would be if I were the new owner. And with you to run the place as always, he must be laughing.'

'I don't know about that,' she said ruefully. 'I haven't seen him laugh yet. He's coming back later to talk properly. Which reminds me, I must get one of the girls to clean through the garden flat. He says he's going to move in there.' She turned back to the buffet. 'This looks lovely, Danny. Get the girls up here ready now, will you? I think I heard some of the golfers go into the bar, so they'll need serving in a minute.'

Happy that the dining-room was all under control, Rowena found Amy the chamber maid about to go off for the afternoon, and asked her to give Donald's flat a quick clean.

'We'll put it down as overtime,'

Rowena said, and the girl happily agreed.

*   *   *

The police asked Rowena to accompany them while they inspected Mr. Harland's room.

'There's no sign of a forced entry,' Sergeant Doller said. 'Anyone could have slipped in if the door was open or if they had a pass key.'

'Or if they'd borrowed the key from behind reception,' added Constable Prout. 'Is the reception desk ever left unattended, Miss Winston?'

Rowena was about to say that such occasions were rare when she remembered that the counter had been left unmanned that morning and said as much to the policeman.

'But it was literally for a matter of minutes,' she added.

'A minute is all it takes,' the sergeant pointed out, and Rowena had to nod in rueful agreement.

'We'd like a word with the chamber maid,' went on Sergeant Doller, and Rowena buzzed the garden flat and asked Amy to come over to the office.

'It wasn't me,' she cried on hearing what had happened. 'It's the man's own fault. He left his key in the door. I found it there. When he hadn't come back by the time I'd finished cleaning his room, I took it down and put it in his pigeon-hole behind the desk.'

'Did you tell the receptionist what you'd done?'

'No. She was there, but she was on the phone. I was getting behind hand so I didn't wait. I just put the key in the pigeon-hole and went back upstairs.'

When this was put to Mr. Harland he looked decidedly uncomfortable and admitted that though he had locked his room once, he had realised halfway downstairs that he'd forgotten his golf shoes. 'I went back up and fetched them. I must have left the key in the door then.'

Rowena was irritated that the man's

carelessness had caused her staff to fall under suspicion, especially as there was now virtually no chance of finding the missing wallet nor of discovering who had taken it.

'Did you dust the room this morning, Amy?' asked Sergeant Doller.

She looked at him indignantly. ''Course I did. Surfaces, mirrors, handles and doors — just like I always do.'

Rowena said, 'And very nice it looked, Amy. I noticed particularly when we were up there just now.'

Amy was slightly mollified. 'Thank you, miss, I do my best.'

'I'm sure you do,' soothed the sergeant. 'Thank you for your help.'

'You mean I can go?'

'Certainly you can.'

'Perhaps you'd just finish the garden flat for me,' said Rowena tactfully. 'Mr. Latimer's hoping to move into it later this afternoon.'

'Of course, miss,' said Amy. 'I've nearly done.'

* * *

Rowena saw the policemen to their car.

'It might be a good idea, Miss Winston, to remind your guests that they are encouraged to leave any valuables or large sums of money in your safe. Perhaps, too, you could keep your eyes open for anything which might help us catch the thief — anyone hanging about or in the wrong place at the wrong time.'

'Yes, of course,' she agreed, but thought privately that it was extremely unlikely any thief would be careless enough to be caught like that.

By the time Clive Latimer returned to the hotel, the early evening reception for the golfing society was in full swing. The terrace room where private functions were held was alive with conversation and laughter.

The waitresses moved from group to group offering drinks and appetisers and Rowena, wearing one of the elegant dresses that she always adopted for evening functions, moved quietly about the room to ensure that all was going smoothly. She saw Clive standing in the doorway of the terrace room surveying the convivial scene and on impulse went over to the golfing society's secretary.

'Mr. Hardiman, do let me introduce you to the new owner of Chalford Manor. You may remember that Mr. Donald Latimer died recently. The club and hotel now belong to Mr. Clive Latimer, his brother.'

Rowena led Hardiman across the room as she spoke and introduced him to Clive.

'Mr. Hardiman's society have been to us several times, Mr. Latimer,' she explained, and then left them to talk, hoping that Hardiman would give them all a good reference.

It was as the golfers were drifting into the bar for a final nightcap, the dinner over and the prizes presented, that Clive approached Rowena again.

'I'm sure you're tired, Miss Winston,'

he said, 'but I would be grateful if you could give me a few moments of your time before you go to bed.'

He sounded polite and conciliatory. Looking up sharply Rowena found no trace of the dislike and distrust she had seen on his face earlier in the day.

'Certainly, Mr. Latimer. I'll be with you in a few minutes,' she replied.

'Fine. I'll be in the flat — just come over when you're ready.' And before she could reply Clive limped away, leaving her staring after him.

In fact it was a good twenty minutes later that Rowena was able to leave the main hotel and cross over to the garden flat. She chose to go by way of the garden rather than approach the flat through the hotel. It gave her a chance to pause for breath in the cool night air. As she leant for a moment on the stone wall that edged the terrace and looked out over the garden, she had to admit to herself that she was not looking forward to the forthcoming interview, particularly as it was to be in Donald's flat. She had not been back into it since the day she had found the unsigned Will and now she had to visit an intruder there. Stupid to think of him as an intruder, it was obvious that he should be free to use the flat, but her dislike of Clive made her feel, irrationally, that he should not be there.

'You know, you look really stunning in that shade of green.'

* * *

Barry's voice sent her spinning round. He caught her by the shoulders and, with her back against the terrace wall, Rowena was not able to move away from him. Letting his eyes rove over her, he went on, 'You really are an attractive woman, Ro, especially by moonlight.' And before she could reply he bent his head and kissed her, holding her firmly to him as she struggled to push him away.

To be so thoroughly kissed twice in one day, having avoided any such contact for years, made Rowena angry and confused. At last he released her and she pulled away, saying with all the cold dignity she could muster, 'Thanks, Barry. That puts me on a par with Beryl.'

He chuckled. 'No comparison,' he said. 'She didn't pretend she didn't like it. She let go and really enjoyed herself.'

At this Rowena turned on her heel without comment. Seeing he had gone too far, Barry caught her arm.

'Rowena, I'm sorry — I shouldn't have said that. It's just I've wanted to kiss you for so long. I thought you liked me.'

'I did.'

'Did?'

'I don't like being mauled, Barry.'

'I'm sorry, Ro, really. Forgive me?' Even as he apologised, Rowena could hear the laughter in his voice. She looked at him warily. 'I suppose so,' she replied, not very graciously.

He grinned and slowly raised her hand to his lips with mock solemnity.

'Barry, you're incorrigible,' she said with a reluctant laugh.

'I know,' he said. 'Fun, isn't it?'

'Are you going to keep me waiting much longer?' Clive's voice had an edge of barely controlled anger as it cut through the darkness. Rowena looked over her shoulder and saw him silhouetted in the light of the garden flat doorway. How long he had been standing there she could not say but in a wave of mortification she felt certain he had watched the whole scene.

Barry dropped her hand. 'Didn't realise I was keeping you from someone else. Good night, Ro.' Then he vanished into the shadows, leaving Rowena to cross the terrace to the garden flat.

Earlier in the day she had been relieved that Clive Latimer had not caught one of the waitresses in Barry Short's ever open arms; now, far worse, she had been caught there herself. Inwardly she cursed both men, one for initiating the incident and the other for witnessing it.

Clive continued to wait in the doorway, only stepping aside as she actually reached him.

'Come in,' he said abruptly, and closed the door behind her.

She stood for a moment in the familiar living-room; she had seen it so often like this, the velvet curtains drawn across the windows, the polished furniture mellow in the lamplight. Everything was exactly as it had always been and yet now it was all quite different. Rowena felt a stab of loneliness as she found herself suddenly accepting that Donald would never come back.

Clive, who had been crossing to the drinks cabinet, suddenly felt her still-ness. Looking across at her he saw the pain in her eyes. For an instant the capable, rather fiery Miss Winston was gone, leaving a beautiful and strangely vulnerable Rowena in her place. He turned abruptly from the sight. With his attention fixed firmly on the contents of the drinks cabinet, he said, 'Do sit down, Miss Winston. Can I get you a drink?'

Rowena sat down in one of Donald's deep armchairs, and said quietly, 'No, thank you, Mr. Latimer.'

Ignoring this, he poured two generous brandies and carried one across to her. When he walked without his stick, his limp was even more pronounced. Rowena noticed that he gave an involuntary grimace of pain when he seated himself in a chair opposite her.

★   ★   ★

Although she had refused a drink, she was actually quite glad of the brandy he had given her. She was tense and tired, and she had a strong suspicion that there were more obstacles to overcome. She looked across at the man opposite her and saw with some surprise that he, too, looked pale and drawn, with lines of fatigue about his eyes.

For a moment he looked much older, almost as old as Donald himself though clearly he must be at least twenty years younger. She wondered, too, what caused him to limp. Obviously his leg pained him but she felt instinctively that he was not a man to give in. He would fight the pain and inconvenience all the way.

'He'll probably fight me all the way, too,' she thought, but even as the thought formed in her mind Clive looked across at her and said, 'I owe you an apology, Rowena. I've been to see David Kelland and he explained the situation to me.'

She opened her mouth to speak but Clive went on quickly, 'Please hear me out. I don't find apologies easy.'

Rowena subsided and took a quick sip of her brandy, allowing him to continue.

'Kelland explained to me how much you had done to help Donald get this place on its feet. He told me all about how you've run it almost single-handed for some time now, and how you had several ideas for expansion and improvement which Donald actually refused to let you implement.

'He explained you had become a partner in everything but name and that he was convinced Donald's not signing that Will was a complete accident — that he truly intended to and simply forgot that he hadn't. So, I apologise for the insinuations I made this morning. Would you reconsider giving in your notice?' he continued. 'Kelland assures me I can't run the place without you, and having seen you at work this evening I'm inclined to believe he's right.'

* * *

Rowena was stunned. It was the last thing she had imagined Clive Latimer was going to say. The apology, though stiff, was heartfelt and she recognised only too well the effort it had cost him to make it.

'Thank you, Mr. Latimer. I accept your apology.'

'And will you reconsider your resignation?'

Rowena hesitated a moment, then: 'I think not. I don't feel somehow that we'd work well together, do you? I think it would be far better for you to find a new manager.'

'I see.' He was silent for a moment and to cover her own awkwardness Rowena sipped her drink.

'Well, perhaps you'd consider making your notice two months so that I'll have time to find a suitable person, and you'll have a chance to work with him and show him the ropes.'

Rowena looked across at the man seated in Donald's chair, so like Donald in looks if not in temperament. He returned her gaze steadily, his eyes never wavering from her face.

She was about to turn him down again when, perhaps sensing her refusal, Clive said: 'Look, we started off very badly this morning but I can assure you it will never happen again. I don't know what sort of relationship you had with my brother — we were, are you know, at best extremely distant. I won't bore you with the reasons, they go way back, that doesn't matter now. But I'd like us to start again, as if we were meeting for the first time now. Can we do that?'

His eyes never left her face and Rowena felt almost trapped by his gaze. She took a long swig of her drink and said, 'If that's what you want, but I'm afraid my notice still stands. You may take it as two months if necessary, but certainly no longer.'

A faint smile twitched Clive's lips and he said, 'Fair enough, then. Perhaps you could set aside some time tomorrow for us to have a detailed discussion about things. I want to know exactly how this place runs.'

'Of course,' she replied formally. 'I'll be in my office most of the morning.'

She set her glass down and got to her feet. 'Now, if you'll excuse me, I'm going to bed. It really has been an extremely long day.'

* * *

Clive pulled himself out of his chair. Rowena noticed another wince of pain as he did so, and realised that his face seemed suddenly grey with fatigue.

'Have you got everything you need?' she asked with sudden concern. 'All Donald's things are still here. I hadn't got round to clearing out the flat, as you can see.'

He nodded wearily. 'Yes, I'll be fine.'

Picking up his stick he escorted her to the door that led through to the hotel.

Impulsively, she said, 'Your leg seems to be very painful. Did you have an accident or something?'

'I've been in hospital for the last month, so I only found your letter when I got home.'

Rowena stared at him. 'You mean that's why you didn't . . . ' Her voice trailed away.

Clive finished the sentence for her. 'Come to his funeral? Yes, that's why.'

Rowena felt the colour drain from her face as she recalled what she had said to him that morning.

'Then I owe you an apology, too,' she said softly.

Again the fleeting smile before Clive said, 'Seems to be a night for apologies. Truce?'

Rowena smiled ruefully and nodded.

'Good,' he said in a satisfied voice. 'Good night, Rowena.'

'Good night, Mr. Latimer.' And with her mind in confusion, Rowena went quietly through the darkened hotel up to her own room under the eaves.

3

Tired as she was, Rowena only slept fitfully that night. As she dozed, images of Donald and Clive and even Barry intruded upon her so that her dreams were a confusion of faces, words and emotions. When she finally awoke it was still very early, but the bright morning sun pierced the crack between her curtains and cast dancing shadows on the wall above her bed.

On impulse she decided to go for a walk before breakfast. It would help clear her head, and she had the feeling that clear-headedness would be all important today.

She dressed quickly and made her way down through the still quiet hotel to the front door.

'You're up early, Miss Winston,' old Jack Parsons, the night porter, remarked as he unlocked the front door for her.

Rowena smiled at him. 'I've got a long day in the office ahead of me,' she said. 'I thought a breath of fresh air might do me good.'

Outside she paused for a moment to breathe in the fresh morning air, and then set off round the house to the garden and the golf course beyond.

Chalford Manor had been built over two hundred years before, an elegant redbrick building with a white stone portico sheltering the front door. A high brick wall continued the line of the building from each wing of the house, one side linking with the garden flat and the other with the stable block. Sheltered behind this wall on the stable side was a huge conservatory which soaked in sunshine for most of the day. Rowena had, at one time, had great ideas for that old conservatory but Donald had not been enthusiastic and her plans had been shelved. She wondered now, as she paused to run her eye over the old glass building, whether it was worth mentioning her idea to Clive. She could not suppress the thought that if only Donald had remembered to sign his Will such a decision would have been hers to take . . .

But though the loss of her inheritance still hurt, Rowena was not one to let self-pity overwhelm her. She turned abruptly away from the conservatory and strode across the sloping lawn, past the tennis courts and on to the golf course beyond. Walking briskly she decided to follow the path which led round the perimeter until she reached the far side and then cut back through the copse in the middle of the course. It was a walk which normally took about half-an-hour.

Dew still spangled the grass and glistened on the hedgerow spiders' webs. The air was fresh and clean and early bird song was the only sound to break the silence. At the turn in the hedge, sheltered by a stand of young oaks, stood Barry's cottage.

'His garden needs attention,' Rowena thought as she approached. She was just wondering if she should broach the matter with him when his back door opened and someone slipped out, closing the door softly behind her. Rowena was surprised but it never crossed her mind to conceal herself and so it was that she reached the gate that led from the cottage garden on to the golf course at the same time as the woman who had just left it. For a moment they stared at each other in surprised recognition.

'Well, Beryl,' said Rowena with a composure she was far from feeling, 'you're up early.'

The waitress paled for a moment and then, with a toss of her fluffy curls, said insolently, 'So are you, Miss Winston. He's awake if you want to see him.' She jerked her head in the direction of the cottage and then darted back towards the hotel.

★   ★   ★

Rowena glanced tight-lipped at the blank cottage windows. A quick kiss in the pavilion with a pretty young waitress was one thing; having her spend the night with him was quite another. She found herself feeling relieved that Barry's contract only ran until the end of September. She'd think very carefully before employing him or anyone like him next summer. 'But, of course,' she thought with a jolt, 'I shan't be here next summer. It won't be my problem.'

'You're about bright and early.' Clive's voice interrupted her cogitations and made her jump. 'Couldn't you sleep?'

'Oh, yes,' she said falsely cheerful, 'but I do like a breath of fresh air before a day in the office, particularly on a morning like this.'

They had agreed a truce and Rowena consciously kept her voice pleasant even as she realised the extent of her loss to him.

'It's a good idea,' he remarked. 'I'll

probably have a stroll myself before I join you in the office. I'm not up to striding round the golf course, though. A quiet wander round the garden will have to do.'

Rowena was startled. How did he know where she'd been? But she kept up her façade of affability and said she must go in for breakfast and would see him later.

Clive nodded and limped back towards the garden flat's door and Rowena went inside, strangely unsettled by the encounter.

She had been at her desk for some time when there was a knock on her office door. Assuming it was Clive, Rowena called 'Come in', and was surprised to see Barry entering, pushing the door to behind him.

Remembering her anger at his behaviour with Beryl, Rowena said rather irritably, 'Is it important, Barry? I've got Mr. Latimer coming to go over the books directly.'

'And you don't want to be caught

gossiping with the staff. Don't worry, I won't keep you long.'

'Well?' she set down her pen and looked across the desk at him. 'What is it?'

'Just a small matter. I understand you were out walking early.'

'And?'

'And that you met Beryl.'

'Yes.' Rowena remained blank-faced.

'Well, poor girl, she's very worried you might report her to Mr. Latimer and she might lose her job.'

'Is she now?' said Rowena coldly. 'That's really none of Mr. Latimer's business. I'm still the manager, so I still do the hiring and firing.'

'Is that a warning, Rowena?'

She looked at him and saw, despite his smile, that there was an unpleasant look in his eyes.

'It wasn't intended as such,' she replied coolly, 'but you can take it as one if you wish.'

There was a moment's silence before Barry laughed. 'Come on, Ro, I'm only joking. Let the poor girl off the hook and tell her you won't fire her just because she came visiting me early this morning.'

'I shan't say anything,' said Rowena, getting up from the desk and opening the window. 'You can tell her yourself. I shan't sack her, though that certainly doesn't mean I approve of her behaviour or yours. But so long as her work isn't affected, her private life is her own business.'

'You're sounding quite stuffy in your old age,' Barry remarked.

Rowena was stung by his comment. 'Talking of old age,' she snapped, 'Beryl is only eighteen. You must be nearly twice as old as she is and you should know better than to encourage her. If you must have an affair, choose someone a little nearer your own age, someone who knows what she's doing.'

'Like you, you mean,' he growled, and with a sudden movement gripped Rowena's wrist and jerked her into his arms.

'Let me go,' she hissed, struggling to free herself. But Barry was too strong for her. All the familiar revulsion flooded through Rowena as he held her captive, but she realised that the more she struggled the more tightly he crushed her to him so she forced herself to relax.

Still holding her firmly, he lifted his head a little to murmur, 'That's better, sweetheart. Just relax and enjoy yourself,' before kissing her again.

'I'm sorry to interrupt you,' said an icy voice from behind them, 'but we have a lot of work to get through, Miss Winston.'

* * *

At the sound of Clive's voice Barry loosened his grasp a little and Rowena was finally able to break away. She turned to see the contempt in Clive's eyes as he came right into the room, leaning heavily on his stick.

Barry, who seemed entirely unabashed,

gave her a casual wave. 'See you later, sweetheart,' he said, before sauntering out of the office.

For one brief moment Rowena considered trying to explain the scene Clive had interrupted, but dismissed the idea immediately. It would be pointless; explanations would sound like excuses and only make the situation worse. Taking deep breaths to help quell her rage at Barry's behaviour, and her dismay at being seen again in such compromising circumstances by Clive, Rowena moved back behind the desk as if to put it between her and recrimination.

But Clive made no reference to what had occurred. Settling himself into a chair, he said: 'Now, first of all I'd like to see one of our brochures so that I get a guest's eye view of the facilities and attractions Chalford Manor has to offer.'

Rowena took her cue from him and their meeting began in earnest.

★ ★ ★

They spent the whole of the rest of the day in her office, going over every aspect of both the hotel and the country club. They did not even break for lunch but had sandwiches and coffee sent up from the kitchen.

She was surprised at how quickly Clive grasped the essentials of her work, and was kept on her toes answering the pertinent and penetrating questions he directed at her.

He studied the accounts and asked about bookings. He was interested in the special deals the hotel offered in the line of activity holidays, conferences, private functions and out of season weekend bargains. When they finally laid aside the papers they had been working on, Clive was clearly impressed with Rowena's organisational and administrative skills. Much of the information he required she could produce from her head, but if a fact or figure eluded her she was immediately able to put her hand on the relevant file.

His eyes held a warmth and respect which had been lacking earlier in the day as he said at last, 'You and Donald have done remarkably well building all this up, you know, it really is a going concern. But I'm a little surprised there have been so few innovations recently. The tennis coaching is the only new attraction introduced in the last two years. It looks to me as if it's about time we tried something new. Any ideas?'

'There were one or two things I was — ' she began, and then stopped awkwardly.

'That you were going to try when the place was yours,' Clive finished for her.

'I was going to say,' said Rowena coldly, 'that I was hoping to persuade Donald to try out.'

'All right, all right. But Kelland told me that you were the innovator in recent years and that Donald tended to hold back. So, what can you come up with?'

'Well,' she began, settling back in her seat. 'There is one idea I'm quite keen on, though I haven't costed it out recently. I'll admit that when I put it to Donald he was less than enthusiastic, but I still think it would work.'

'What is it?'

'It'll be easier if I show you,' she said. 'Come on.'

She led Clive out into the garden and round to the conservatory on the southern wall. Opening the door, they went inside. The sun had been shining on the glass all day and had raised the temperature to almost tropical heights.

'We've never done anything with this place,' Rowena explained. 'There's a vine growing along the back, but it's not been looked after and produces very few grapes. At one time Donald wanted to use it as a greenhouse to grow fresh vegetables for the hotel kitchen, but it proved uneconomic when we looked into it and the idea was dropped.' She gazed round at the forlorn glasshouse. The outside had been painted so that it did not spoil the overall appearance of the hotel, but the inside had been sadly neglected.

Clive looked round without enthusiasm.

'And what do you suggest we use it for now?'

'I thought that with careful alteration it could be made to house a small indoor swimming pool. I envisage it with white tables and chairs set around and some big indoor plants in tubs — a place where people can sit and watch the swimmers. Even in the winter it gets quite warm in here, and of course the pool itself would be heated. On the other side of that wall are the locker rooms where the members change for tennis and golf. It's actually the men's locker room there but there's nothing to stop us putting up some stud partitioning and creating a narrow corridor to the ladies' locker room beyond, so changing cubicles would be no problem.'

She turned back to Clive, her face alight with enthusiasm, and found him gazing at her in admiration.

'You really have got it worked out, haven't you?' he asked.

★   ★   ★

Rowena was immediately on the defensive. 'Well, you did ask me,' she said coolly.

'I did,' agreed Clive. 'And I haven't finished asking you yet. I can see that this idea has possibilities, but think of a day like today. It's an oven in here now. Even with a pool to dip into, I wouldn't want to sit in here for long.'

'I've thought of that,' she began.

'I thought you might have,' murmured Clive, and seeing her about to protest again said hastily: 'Go on, I'm listening.'

'Well, the roof is held up by three main supports and in between it is simply wooden framing and glass. I think it would be comparatively easy to take out the central section between those two pillars — ' she waved her hand in the direction of the glass walls

— 'and replace them with big sliding doors. Then, on hot days, they could be pulled open and it would almost be like swimming in an outdoor pool. We could build a small terrace outside and have some all-weather tables and chairs out there so that people can move out into the sun if they want to.'

'What size pool are you talking of?' asked Clive. Rowena glanced at him sharply but there was no hint of mockery in his face now.

'We wouldn't need anything too big,' she replied. 'But it would be better to have one which is an interesting shape rather than a plain rectangle. It makes the place far more attractive, don't you think?'

'Get some quotes in, Rowena, get it costed out and let me have detailed figures as soon as you can. I shall be away for a week or so from tomorrow so see if you can have something for me when I get back.'

Rowena was startled at his sudden decision. Donald would have taken weeks to chew over the idea before he even expressed enough interest to cost the project out. Physically Donald and Clive were alike but the similarity stopped there. Even when he had first bought Chalford Manor and employed Rowena as his assistant, Donald had never had the energy and decisiveness which characterised his brother. She was delighted with Clive's reaction to her scheme and gave no heed to the thought that she would no longer be at Chalford Manor if and when it actually became a reality.

'All right, Mr. Latimer,' she began.

'Clive,' he interjected. 'If we're going to work together, even if only for a couple of months, I'd find it much easier if you addressed me as Clive.'

'If you like,' she agreed. 'Anyway, I'll have it all ready for you when you come back. A week, you said?'

'Give or take a day or so. I've other things to attend to.' He swung round towards the conservatory door as he spoke. One moment he was standing up, the next he had fallen with a sharp cry of pain. She was beside him in an instant and as she knelt beside him saw his face contort with pain. He must have fallen on the uneven brick flooring, and his injured knee had been brought into sharp contact with an old stone water trough. For a moment he closed his eyes, grasping Rowena's extended hands so tightly that she felt her fingers would be crushed. Then, as the worst of the pain subsided, Clive relaxed his grip. He opened his eyes and saw Rowena's concern for him.

'Sorry, missed my footing,' he said with a weak smile.

'We must get you to the flat,' she said gently. 'Will you be all right for a minute while I go for some help? Barry's sure to be on the tennis courts.'

'No,' he snapped, adding more calmly, 'No, I can manage with my stick if you could just give me a shoulder to lean on.'

She looked doubtful. 'Well, all right, if you're sure.' Gently she freed her hands which he still held in his and got to her feet. She retrieved his walking stick and then supported him as he heaved himself up from the ground. She waited as he regained his balance and then together they left the conservatory and made their slow progress across the terrace to the garden flat.

★   ★   ★

Once inside, Rowena eased Clive into an armchair and drew across a footstool so that he could rest his leg on it.

'Can I do anything else?' she said. 'Have you any pain killers?'

'By the bed,' he said weakly.

She found a bottle of prescription pain killers beside the bed. She went into the little kitchen for a glass of water and at the same time put the kettle on, then returned to Clive. There was a tinge of colour in his face and she handed him the pain killers and water.

'I've put the kettle on for tea,' she said.

'I'd rather have a large brandy,' he grumbled.

'Perhaps you would, but large brandies don't go with pain killers.'

'You are an extremely bossy woman,' Clive complained.

'I know. That's why I'm so good at my job.'

'Yes,' he acknowledged, suddenly serious. 'Yes, you're right. You do it very well.'

She was embarrassed to feel the sudden colour flooding her face at his compliment and said quickly, 'I'll just go and make that tea.'

When she carried the tray into the room Clive had taken the pills and was lying back with his eyes closed. He forced them open as he heard her come in.

'You know,' she remarked, passing him a cup, 'you don't look fit to be going anywhere tomorrow.'

He grinned ruefully. 'I've got to go — my physiotherapy starts then. Don't worry, I'll be all right. I've got a car coming to pick me up as I can't drive again yet, so I'll be dropped at the door. My knee was feeling much better until I fell on it just now. Really, I'll be all right. You just have those figures ready for when I get back, and we ought to look more closely at security then as well.'

'Yes, I am rather worried about that,' admitted Rowena.

'Well, see if you can come up with some ideas in that direction, too.'

Rowena got to her feet. 'I'll try,' she said. 'Now what'll you do about supper? Shall I ask Danny to send you over a tray?'

'Would you?' Clive looked up at her gratefully. 'That would be just the thing.'

'And you really won't take any alcohol now you've had those pills, will you?'

Clive gave a wry smile. 'No,' he promised. 'I won't.'

Rowena left him then and, having arranged for Danny to send him some supper, sought the sanctuary of her own rooms.

Rowena had a little flatlet on the very top floor of the hotel. Further along the corridor were the bedrooms used by other staff who lived in but Rowena's flat consisted of a bedroom looking out across the golf course and a small sitting-room with a view down the drive. A shower-room and kitchenette completed the suite and meant that she had a tiny but completely self-contained home.

Although she had had only a sandwich lunch, she found she was not hungry and contented herself with a bowl of soup and some toast. It was as she finally began to relax over her supper that Rowena suddenly realised that at no time during the half hour she had spent in the garden flat had she given Donald so much as a passing thought. Already, she realised guiltily, she thought of it as Clive's flat.

'Oh Donald, I do miss you,' she cried aloud. And then, illogically, she added in a whisper: 'And I wish you hadn't hated Clive.'

4

Clive left Chalford Manor immediately after breakfast. Apart from a brief: 'Goodbye, I'll be back some time next week' to Rowena when he met her in the hall, she had no conversation with him before he went and he was soon out of her thoughts as she concentrated on the day's work.

One of her first jobs was to ring a swimming pool contractor to get him to send someone to look into the feasibility of her conservatory plan. She was determined to get the scheme launched as soon as possible and made the appointment for the next day.

Gilly reminded her that she was to attend a meeting of the Country Club Social Committee in the evening to discuss the arrangements for the annual midsummer ball; that on top of her normal routine work meant she was in

88

for another long day.

She did not see Barry at all, and was pleased. She had been very angry at his behaviour of the last few days. She had realised that he had an eye for the women soon after he had arrived, and had said as much to Donald, but she disliked intensely his attention being turned in her direction. She determined to steer well clear of him from now on, keeping any unavoidable contact at a strictly business level, but that proved to be more easily said than done.

It was the next day, as she stood chatting to the pool contractor in the drive, that Barry approached her again. Coming round from the tennis courts he saw them standing together and immediately strolled across to join them. Rowena was glad the man had come in a car not a company van for she did not want her plans to become generally known until it was certain that they would go ahead.

Luckily the pool man was about to

leave and Rowena hastened his departure as Barry came over by saying, 'Give me a ring when you've done some costings, and if I like what I hear you can do me a detailed written estimate.'

'Right you are,' said the man, and with a brief 'Good afternoon' to Barry, got into his car and drove off.

'Who was that?' he asked with a grin. 'What project are you on now?'

'None of your business,' said Rowena firmly, turning back towards the hotel. 'Now, if you'll excuse me, Barry, I've got . . . '

'Hang on a minute, Ro,' he cried. 'Don't dash off. I just wanted a word.'

She paused. 'Well?' she said discouragingly.

Barry treated her to his most devastating smile. 'I just wanted to apologise.'

'Oh, yes?'

'Yes,' he insisted. 'I really am very sorry for the way I behaved the other day. I'd no right to force myself on you like that.' He gave a deprecatory little laugh. 'Though most women seem to like it . . . '

'I'm not most women,' she said sharply.

'I know. That's the trouble. Still,' he hurried on as she began to saunter back to the hotel, 'it won't happen again, I promise you. I really am very sorry.'

Rowena stopped and looked at him. With a sigh and an unwilling smile at the consternation on his face, she said, 'It's all right, Barry, forget it.'

He beamed at her. 'You mean that?' he asked.

'Yes, of course,' she replied briskly. 'Now I really must . . . '

'Then have a drink with me this evening. Or we could play tennis, like before.'

Rowena looked at him in mild exasperation. 'I haven't time for tennis,' she said. 'I've an appointment at seven, but I'll meet you in the bar later if you like, about half-past eight.'

As soon as she'd said it she began to regret the promise. But when she finally did go down to the bar, Barry was waiting, smiling, with her drink ready for her at a table in the corner.

At first their chat was general, but inevitably it came round to the arrival of Clive Latimer.

'It's funny,' remarked Barry, 'it never dawned on me that it might be *the* Clive Latimer. I mean, Donald was so much older, you wouldn't have thought that they were brothers.'

Rowena stared at him. 'What do you mean?' she asked. '*The* Clive Latimer?'

Now it was Barry's turn to stare. 'You mean you haven't recognised him?'

Rowena shook her head. 'No, should I?'

'I'd have thought so, but perhaps not. He hasn't been headline news for several years now, I suppose.' He gave a bitter laugh. 'How short is the memory of the fickle public!'

'Barry, what are you talking about?'

demanded Rowena.

'Clive Latimer — Davis Cup player and quarter-finalist at Wimbledon.'

'What?'

'Don't you remember? A great British hope until the accident.'

'I remember the name,' she began.

'But not the face,' Barry finished for her. 'Well, I suppose I shouldn't be surprised. It's only the very top players who are instantly recognised, especially after so long.'

'You mean that this is the Clive Latimer everyone was so excited about — when was it? — about eight years ago. Are you sure?'

Barry nodded. 'Of course. It's my sport, remember. I knew as soon as I saw him in your office the other day.'

'But you didn't say anything.'

'It hardly seemed the appropriate time,' he said with a grin, and Rowena suddenly remembered the circumstances.

'But I've forgotten what happened to him,' she said. 'I mean, why didn't he keep playing tennis if he was so good?'

'There was an accident,' Barry replied. 'A car smash. I don't remember the details, but I think his legs were crushed, or one leg or something. Anyway, it put him out of the big time for good.'

'How awful,' breathed Rowena. 'What a dreadful thing to happen.'

'He was luckier than his passenger,' Barry said with a shrug. 'I seem to remember she was killed — outright or died in hospital.'

'Who was she?'

Barry shrugged again. 'Can't remember her name,' he said, 'but I think it was his fiancée. Women always swarmed round him; it was certainly a girl and I think they were engaged. Anyway, she was killed in the crash and he was just injured.'

'What a terrible thing,' Rowena thought. She was about to make the remark out loud when she saw that Barry's face was entirely devoid of sympathy, so said instead: 'I suppose that's why he limps now. Do you think it's the same injury?'

'Could be.' He seemed to have lost interest in the whole subject. 'When are we going to play tennis again, Ro?' he queried. 'Even with a new boss you're entitled to some time off.'

Rowena smiled. 'I don't know, perhaps tomorrow evening?'

'Well, I've Celia Morton-Harvey coming for a lesson at six, but after that would be fine.'

'Are you sure?' said Rowena. 'About Mrs. Morton-Harvey, I mean?'

Barry looked at her sharply and said, 'As far as I know, why?'

'Well, it's just that I had a letter from her this morning resigning from the club.'

'What?' Barry sounded incredulous. 'But she was coming along so nicely. What reason did she give?'

Rowena shook her head. 'None. She just said that the family would not be renewing their membership when it fell due in June.'

'Perhaps she's joined another club,' suggested Barry.

'I suppose she must have,' said Rowena. 'It's a pity, she was always such an efficient member of the social committee, she and Angela Thomas. We shall miss them.'

'Angela Thomas? Has she resigned, too?'

Rowena nodded. 'They both resigned from the committee last night, I gather. It's a great pity with the midsummer ball coming up. Still, I expect we'll manage.'

'Blow the midsummer ball,' wailed Barry in dismay, 'they're two of my star pupils. I must be wearing the wrong flavour aftershave.'

*　*　*

Rowena laughed and got to her feet. 'Don't blame your aftershave now,' she said, 'but I'm going to have to go.'

'One more drink?' he asked hopefully but she shook her head.

'No,' she said firmly. 'I must have an early night. But I'll see you tomorrow evening for our tennis, if you're still on for that.'

'Yes, of course.' He escorted her to the lift in the front hall. 'See you tomorrow, then. Good night.'

He raised a hand in salute, and as the lift gates closed turned towards the front door. He had kept his promise and hadn't so much as touched her hand. Their earlier friendship seemed to be restored and Rowena was relieved.

Later, as she lay in bed trying to sleep, she found herself turning over in her mind what Barry had told her about Clive Latimer. Eight years ago she would have been just eighteen, about to leave school. How old would Clive have been? Twenty-three, perhaps; that would make him thirty-one now, twenty-four years younger than Donald. It really was a surprising difference in their ages. And poor Clive with his promising career cut short by a dreadful car smash! Was that when

Donald and Clive had fallen out? Obviously they could never have been close as brothers because of the age difference, but when did the real rift occur?

Still wondering, Rowena drifted into sleep.

Next evening she was surprised to see that Celia Morton-Harvey had, after all, had her lesson with Barry. As Rowena strolled across to the courts she saw them feeding tennis balls into the machine. It was a moment before Barry saw her, but when he did he waved cheerfully. Mrs. Morton-Harvey turned quickly and, seeing Rowena dressed for tennis, walked towards the gate.

'See you next week, Mrs. Morton-Harvey,' called Barry to her departing back. 'And don't forget what I said — keep practising that serve.'

Mrs. Morton-Harvey did not reply. Her heavily made-up face looked mask-like and there was a strange, bleak expression upon it.

'We're all so sorry you'll be leaving the club, Mrs. Morton-Harvey,' said Rowena as they met at the gate.

'Yes, well, it's just one of those things. A necessity, I'm afraid. Good night, Rowena.'

Rowena watched her go, wondering if the family had run into financial trouble. The subscription to the country club was certainly not cheap, even at the special family rate which applied to the Morton-Harveys, but they never appeared to be short of money.

'She seemed a bit depressed,' Rowena remarked to Barry as they began knocking up. 'Did she say anything to you?'

'Not a word,' Barry answered cheerfully. 'Probably just having a bad day.'

Rowena felt there was more to it than that but she put the subject from her mind and concentrated on her game as Barry kept her on her toes about the court. It was good to play against someone so much better than herself, even if he did grin roguishly as he frequently placed the ball just out of her reach. By the end of their game she was exhausted, gasping for the shandy Barry brought out to the terrace. She was about to go up to her flat to shower and change when Gilly appeared on the terrace, looking for her.

'Rowena, please could you come? Some more money's gone missing.'

Rowena got up wearily. 'Yes, of course.' She turned to Barry. 'Sorry, I'll have to go. Thanks for the game.'

'Anything I can do?' he volunteered, getting up.

'No, I doubt it, thanks all the same.' Rowena followed the agitated Gilly into the hotel to deal with the matter.

* * *

Mrs. Gardener and Mrs. Drake who had been playing tennis on one of the other courts were waiting at reception. 'I'm sorry, Rowena,' Mrs. Drake said. 'It's my own fault, really, I suppose. I took my handbag on to the court with me as usual but I'd forgotten that I'd left my purse in my grip with my clothes. Anyway, when I came in, the grip had been emptied on to the floor and my purse is missing.'

'And my watch,' put in Mrs. Gardener. 'I left it in my shoe.'

By the time the whole affair had been dealt with, the police informed and statements had been made, it was quite late. At last Rowena was able to take her shower and change into more comfortable clothes, but she did not then spend the rest of the evening relaxed in front of her television as she'd planned but went back into her office. Here she spent a further hour making copious notes for Clive on how the hotel security worked and how it might be tightened up.

'Though,' she thought as she finally closed the file and left the office, 'whatever we do will make little difference if people leave their watches in their shoes while they're out on the tennis court!'

* * *

Clive Latimer did not return to Chalford Manor for two weeks. He telephoned once to warn Rowena that a van would be arriving with some personal belongings and asked her to have them delivered straight into the garden flat.

'Any problems?' he enquired casually, and on hearing Rowena's assurances that there were none said, 'I'll see you next week, then,' and rang off.

Rowena had decided not to mention the thieving again until she had Clive face-to-face and she could more easily gauge his reactions. Nor did she mention the growing file she was compiling on the conversion of the conservatory; she wanted to be able to present him with a complete dossier.

It was while she was working on some of the figures for the swimming pool that Gilly knocked and said, 'Mrs. Morton-Harvey wondered if you could spare her a few moments.'

Rowena placed the papers on which she was working in a file and said, 'Of course, ask her to come in.'

When Mrs. Morton-Harvey appeared Rowena noticed again how pale she looked, even under her heavy make-up. Her eyes seemed shadowed and tired and her smile unnaturally forced.

Rowena settled her into a chair and asked, 'How can I help you, Mrs. Morton-Harvey?'

Celia Morton-Harvey shifted uncomfortably, clearly ill-at-ease.

'It's about my letter of resignation,' she began, and then stopped.

'What about it?' prompted Rowena.

'What have you done with it?'

'Nothing as yet,' Rowena replied. 'It'll go up before the general committee next week and then they will invite someone near the top of the waiting list to take over your membership. As you know the club is limited to a certain number and vacancies are very quickly filled.'

Mrs. Morton-Harvey nodded. 'Yes,'

she began. 'I know. It's not an easy club to get into.'

'Had you someone particular you wanted to recommend for your place?' asked Rowena, trying to be helpful. It was obvious the woman across the desk had something on her mind.

For a moment Mrs. Morton-Harvey stared at her dully as if she did not understand the question then she said abruptly, 'Can I withdraw it?'

'I beg your pardon?'

'Can I withdraw our resignation as it hasn't gone before the committee yet? Couldn't you just give me back the letter and forget I ever sent it?'

Rowena looked puzzled. 'Well, I suppose I could,' she said.

'It's just that I sent the resignation without mentioning it to my husband, you see.'

Once she had started her explanation, Mrs. Morton-Harvey's words came tumbling out. 'He was furious. He said we'd regret not being members and that it would take years to get back in. I thought it might not be the same now Mr. Latimer's died, but my husband said nonsense, and was angry I'd resigned. I wondered if I could withdraw our resignation?'

Rowena smiled at her reassuringly. 'I'm sure you can. As I said, it's not official yet. I'll just give you back your letter and there'll be no problem.'

Mrs. Morton-Harvey looked so relieved, she seemed on the verge of tears.

'Oh, Rowena, thank you.' Gone was the rather flirtatious, sophisticated woman Rowena was used to seeing about the club. For a moment she seemed far less self-assured and rather frightened. What of? Rowena wondered. Her husband, perhaps. What a lot of fuss about a club membership.

'I'm afraid you've already been replaced on the social committee,' Rowena told her. 'We had to have the full number to organise the summer ball.'

'Oh, of course, I quite understand,' cried Mrs. Morton-Harvey, her usual condescending expression back in place. 'It'll be quite a relief to come to that simply as a guest and not as an organiser.'

★ ★ ★

Rowena abstracted the letter of resignation from a file and handed it over to Mrs. Morton-Harvey who took it with a gracious 'Thank you so much', and put it in her handbag. Then she rose to her feet and extended her hand to Rowena.

'It was kind of you to see me and help me sort this out. Thank you.' She glided out of the room leaving Rowena wondering at the whole peculiar incident.

It was rendered all the more peculiar the following day when Angela Thomas also asked if she, too, might withdraw her letter of resignation. She went into no detailed explanation but simply said that she had changed her mind and was it too late?

Rowena assured her it wasn't and

restored her letter to her, at which Angela Thomas said 'Thanks, I'm grateful', and disappeared still clutching the letter.

Rowena mentioned it to Barry one evening when they were playing tennis, but he could offer no suggestion as to why either resignation had been tendered in the first place or later withdrawn. He merely shrugged his shoulders. 'Women! Never could understand what passes for their minds.'

Rowena aimed a ball at him but he volleyed it neatly away into a corner and went on: 'Come on, I'll play you for a shandy. Usual handicap.'

Rowena played hard, fighting for every point, but even with a large handicap she wasn't able to beat Barry. As the light faded and seeing the ball became difficult she did succeed in passing him several times at net and felt that although she owed him a pint of shandy she had acquitted herself quite creditably. So, it turned out, did someone else for as they played the final point and met at the net to shake hands there was a round of applause from the side of the court. Rowena turned to see who was there and was surprised to see Clive standing watching.

'That last game was a good one,' he remarked as they walked over to him. Rowena, suddenly remembering who he was, wished he hadn't been there to see her efforts.

'She's coming on well,' said Barry, as if to claim he was coaching her.

'But you still won the pint,' pointed out Rowena, smiling to cover the sudden strange uneasiness she felt as the two men confronted each other. It was not really a confrontation, they simply met at the gate, but the atmosphere was tense nonetheless.

Then the moment passed and Clive said easily, 'Are you busy now, Rowena? If not, I could do with a hand to unpack the things which arrived the other day. They're still stacked up in the sitting-room.'

'Yes, I know — I'm sorry,' she began. 'I didn't know what else to do with them.'

'What a pity,' Barry interrupted rudely, 'but we were just going for a drink. After all, it is Rowena's evening off.'

'I see,' said Clive coldly. 'Well, of course, I shan't interfere with that. I'll see you in the morning then, Rowena. In the office at nine.'

And with that he turned on his heel and stalked away. It wasn't until later as she found herself re-living the brief interchange that Rowena realised that Clive was not using his stick and his limp seemed less pronounced. At the time she was angry with Barry for answering for her.

'I wish you hadn't said that,' she snapped, turning on him. 'I can answer for myself, you know.'

'I'm sure you can,' he agreed smoothly. 'Only you wouldn't have. You'd have trotted after him to do his unpacking, and left me to buy my own shandy.'

Rowena sighed. 'Come on then,' she

said. 'Just a quick one. It isn't really my evening off. I'm due at a general committee meeting in three quarters of an hour.'

'Oh, so you couldn't have rushed to his assistance anyway?'

'No, but I'd have preferred the chance to explain that for myself.'

When the committee meeting was over, Rowena returned to her office before she went up to bed. She wanted a final glance at her swimming pool presentation before she showed it to Clive in the morning. It was all prepared but even so she read it through again just to be sure she had missed nothing. Then she smiled with satisfaction. She was certain Clive would approve the scheme and found herself looking forward to showing it to him in the morning.

* * *

Rowena was in her office well before nine next day, and was pleased she was when Clive appeared at ten minutes to. She knew that he now accepted that her job was no sinecure but even so she found herself strangely on the defensive where he was concerned, and determined he should have no chance to catch her out in unpunctuality or idleness.

'Good morning,' she said as he appeared at the door. She was surprised and mortified to feel a rush of colour to her cheeks and strove to keep her voice even.

'Morning.' Clive advanced into the room and Rowena found herself newly aware of him. Without his stick he seemed taller, his shoulders broader, and the casual checked shirt and navy cord trousers he was wearing emphasised his masculinity. His was the body of an athlete, its power and strength held in check until they should be needed. How could she not have noticed before? Rowena wondered as he dropped easily into the chair she had set ready for him. How could she have remained unaware of the controlled energy of his movements, the restrained grace.

'Is your leg better?' she asked hurriedly. 'You seem to be moving more easily and there's no stick.'

'Yes, a fortnight's physio has worked wonders. Still some way to go yet, but I'll get there in the end.'

Rowena could hear the determination underlying the easy tenor of his voice, but before she could speak again Clive went on smoothly: 'Now then, what's been going on here?'

They spent the whole morning working, their chairs drawn together as they pored over the detailed breakdown of the swimming pool scheme. Rowena found herself continually aware of Clive's proximity. In the course of handling papers and reaching across to point out significant items in her report, their hands and arms touched. Although such contact was entirely unintentional, Rowena was conscious of a growing warmth within her, as if she was drawing heat from Clive, and while he was studying a sheet of figures she took the chance to watch him unobserved. He was clearly better than he had been two weeks earlier. The pallor had gone from his cheeks and the dark shadows from under his eyes. For the first time, she realised, she was really seeing him as Clive instead of Donald's younger brother. She also realised with a start how much thought she had given to him while he had been away.

He glanced up from the estimate and caught her gaze but all he said was, 'This looks good, Rowena. Let's have another look at the plans.'

★   ★   ★

She reached for the scale plans and elevations she had had drawn and spread them over the desk once more. Clive studied them for a moment and then said: 'Fine. Let's get on with it.'

Rowena's eyes lit up. 'You mean that? That we should go ahead?'

'Yes. It's a good scheme and will add a good deal to the club — particularly in the winter.'

Rowena smiled with delight. 'Then I'll put it all in hand,' she said, 'unless, of course, you want to handle it?'

Clive shook his head. 'No. You carry on for now. It's a pity you won't be here to see its completion, but never mind. I'll see you get an invitation to its grand opening.'

His words were like a douche of cold water and Rowena's smile faded. But Clive was apparently unaware of the effect his words had had on her and went on cheerfully: 'You get them started as soon as they can and I'll organise the finance. Now — ' he continued briskly — 'is there anything else you want to discuss, because if not I really ought to go. I have to meet someone in an hour. She'll be staying at the hotel, by the way, so perhaps you'd have a room prepared for her. Her name's Jean, Jean Brewer. She'll be here for a couple of days at least, maybe more.'

'Yes, of course,' Rowena replied automatically. 'I'll speak to Gilly. I did want to have a word with you about security, actually.'

'It'll have to wait,' said Clive tersely. 'I don't want to be late.'

'Yes, of course,' said Rowena again. 'But we must talk some time. And I've done you a file on the Summer Ball. It's one of the big events of the year and Donald always attended.'

'And you think I should? Well, give me both files, I'll take them with me.'

Rowena passed him the two buff-coloured folders and Clive got to his feet.

'We'll try and have another talk tomorrow sometime,' he said. 'I'll let you know when I've planned what I'm doing. See you later.'

Rowena, still sitting at her desk, felt the room grow suddenly empty and cold.

5

The first time Rowena saw Jean Brewer was at dinner that evening, when Clive brought her into the hotel dining-room and they were shown at once to the table Donald had always used. Rowena had glanced in to check on a table that had been booked by a large party and Clive called her across.

'Rowena, this is Jean Brewer, a friend of mine. I thought she might well be interested in taking on your job when you leave us, so I've brought her down for a day or two so she can get the feel of the place.'

'How do you do?' said Rowena automatically while she took in the smooth sweep of Jean Brewer's fair hair, the fashionable cut of her clothes, the immaculate make-up.

Jean inclined her head in answer to Rowena's greeting, and Clive went on,

'Of course you'll be able to give her the lowdown on what the job entails, introduce her to the staff and generally make sure she learns her way about, won't you, Rowena? Explain the projects we're working on, too. Who knows? She might well come up with some fresh ideas of her own. Eh, Jean?'

Jean gave a silvery laugh.

'I haven't decided yet that I *want* to be buried in the country, Clive,' she said, 'but I must say that looking round this place I can see that it has distinct possibilities. With a fresh eye it could really be made into something.' She glanced up at Rowena, adding in a tone which belied her actual words, 'I'm sure you've done a great deal here yourself — please don't think I'm belittling your efforts, Rosemary — '

'Rowena.'

'Rowena. But, of course, after a while even the best of us become stale, and without a steady flow of new ideas a place like this does tend to stagnate, don't you think?'

'I hadn't noticed it,' said Rowena coolly.

'No, precisely. You see what I mean,' returned Jean sweetly. Turning her attention to Clive, she went on, 'I'll be very interested in what Rowena has to show me, Clive, but you will accept that if I agree to take this job on, I'll want a free hand.'

'Of course,' he agreed amiably. 'You're the expert.'

Rowena, sensing she had been forgotten, murmured her excuses and slipped away. As she went out into the hall a backward glance revealed Jean and Clive, their heads close together, sleek blonde beside thick dark hair, laughing companionably together. She felt a wave of anger and despair wash over her: anger at the thought of a woman like Jean Brewer taking over the running of her beloved Chalford Manor, and despair as she realised it was due to her own hasty reaction that it was to be so. If she had not given Clive her notice in her first fury, or even if she had reconsidered when he asked her to do so, the situation would never have arisen.

She went upstairs to find Amy who should now be turning down the beds. As she reached the landing she saw not Amy but Beryl coming out of one of the bedrooms.

'Beryl,' she challenged, 'what are you doing up here? You should be down in the dining-room.'

'Danny sent me up with a tray for number seventeen,' replied Beryl pertly. 'I'm going back down now.'

'I see,' Rowena replied evenly. 'Have you seen Amy? I wanted a word with her.'

'In twenty-one I think,' said Beryl, waving a hand towards an open door further along the corridor, and then walking briskly to the back stairs.

Rowena found Amy and warned her to be particularly careful when doing Jean Brewer's room.

'Make sure that there are plenty of

towels and see that all the other bathroom requisites are there,' she said.

'Of course, Miss Winston. I've checked all that, do you want to see?'

'No, no. It's just that she's a friend of Mr. Latimer's and I don't want her to have any complaints.'

'She shouldn't do, Miss Winston, I done it just like I always do.'

'Of course you have,' soothed Rowena. 'Good night, Amy.' And she went back down to the hall to be on hand when the large party booking arrived. She was in time to see Clive and Jean come out of the dining-room, and to hear Jean say in a rather penetrating voice: 'You see what I mean about the hall, Clive? But it won't be difficult to alter, and it'll make all the difference.'

'That's an extremely clever idea, Jean, I must look into that.' And then they disappeared down the passage towards the garden flat.

* * *

Rowena glanced round the hall to see if she could guess what particular 'improvement' Jean could have had in mind but could see nothing she herself would wish to alter. Indeed, Rowena had always been proud of the entrance hall; it stated the character of the place and she and Donald had given much time and thought to the decoration and the furnishing of it. How dare that woman seek to alter it! Angry again, Rowena went into the bar. Seeing Barry perched on his favourite stool at one end she joined him.

'You look glum,' he remarked. 'Have a drink to cheer you up, and tell me your problems.' He bought her a gin and tonic and suggested they carry them out to the terrace.

The evening air was warm and balmy and they sat on the terrace wall sipping their drinks in companionable silence. The last shafts of evening sunlight pierced the branches of the full-leaved oaks at the lawns' end to dapple the grass beneath. As Rowena let her eyes roam the familiar scene, she felt near to tears at its beauty. How she had come to love Chalford Manor; not just for the happy memories it held nor yet for the pride it gave her to know her part in its development as a hotel and flourishing country club. More than that, its timeless quietude and beauty had crept into her soul.

'I shall miss this place,' she thought with an ache in her heart. 'I shall never forget this view.' And she gazed long and deep as if trying to imprint the image on her mind.

'Penny for them,' said Barry.

Rowena heard his voice but not his words. 'Sorry,' she said. 'What did you say?'

'You were miles away,' he remarked. 'I just asked what you were thinking.'

'Oh, just what a beautiful evening it is,' Rowena replied tightly.

'Let's hope it's like this for the Summer Ball.'

She had been on the verge of telling Barry how much she regretted her decision to leave Chalford but although their friendship seemed to have returned to its even tenor, she could not quite erase from her mind the unpleasant, almost violent side she had seen of him as he had seized her in his arms. Instinctively, she kept her confidences to herself, and kept their conversation light and general until she had to go inside to welcome the dinner party group.

Next morning, when she went into her office, Rowena found Jean Brewer already there with Clive, studying the summer brochure and special events file.

'Good morning,' Rowena said abruptly, fighting to keep a rein on her temper. How dare they go to her desk and filing cabinet? Yet of course Clive had every right to do so and it was this knowledge that made her bite back her anger.

'Ah, Rowena,' he said affably. 'I was just showing Jean some of our projects. Obviously she's keen to see exactly what she'd be taking on.'

'Of course,' said Rowena tightly.

'There seems to be tremendous room for expansion here,' drawled Jean, glancing up from the glossy leaflet she held. 'Including, I'd have thought, doubling the membership.'

'Donald gave considerable thought to the membership limits,' said Rowena. 'If it is thrown open to anyone, the club loses exclusivity and standards drop. At the moment all members feel that there are facilities there for them to enjoy at any time without being overcrowded.'

'I can see that could be an argument,' commented Jean, 'but many of these facilities are under-used. We can't afford to be too fussy as to the type of people we accept.'

'We can't afford not to be,' snapped Rowena. 'We run this club for members and their families to seek their own leisure pursuits; we run the hotel to cater to a more distant clientèle who wish to pay to make use of our facilities. We are not running a holiday camp. The members make the club rules and their committee is elected to do just that.'

'But you're on that committee,' pointed out Jean.

'Ex-officio, yes, but I make no effort to alter the club's constitution.'

'I'm sure it would only be a question of tactfully pointing out the advantages,' purred Jean, and then, before Rowena could reply, she went on, 'You needn't stay, Clive. I'm sure Rowena can tell me all I need to know.'

'Fine,' he agreed. 'I'll see you for lunch in the dining-room at about one?'

'Lovely.' And Jean turned her attention back to Rowena, who clearly had not been included in Clive's invitation.

★ ★ ★

It was the most miserable day Rowena had ever spent. Jean had as much tact and diplomacy as a runaway steam roller and on every subject, ranging from activity holidays through to the rooms provided for live-in staff, she had disparaging comments to make and new ideas to introduce. By the end of the day Rowena felt like a limp rag, but burning inside her was a fierce flame of resentment.

This woman would make a mockery of everything Donald and Rowena had achieved. How could Clive even entertain the idea of employing her to manage Chalford? She might be an adequate businesswoman from a purely financial standpoint, but she had entirely missed the subtleties of Chalford. She might boost the profits for a while, though Rowena considered even that to be doubtful, but she would destroy the place's peaceful ambience in the process. She had even mentioned taking down the firs as they restricted the view.

'I won't let her,' resolved Rowena as she sat by her window that evening, recovering from the day. 'She won't spoil everything we've established.'

She gazed out along the lime avenue and wondered if Jean Brewer would want to cut that down, too. The thought was too much for her and she decided she would approach Clive first thing in the morning. Quite what she would say Rowena wasn't sure, but she did know she wasn't prepared to let Jean Brewer replace her without a fight.

★ ★ ★

She woke late next morning, and by the time she appeared in the hall Gilly had replaced Jack Parsons at the reception desk.

'When Mr. Latimer comes through, would you ask him if he could spare me a few minutes sometime this morning?' Rowena said.

Gilly replied, 'I'm sorry, Rowena, but he's gone already.'

'Gone?'

'He and Miss Brewer left about half-an-hour ago. He said he was going up to London on business but he'd be back in a day or two.'

Rowena felt an angry despair welling inside her. 'I see,' she said. 'I didn't realise he was going so early. Did he

127

leave any message for me?'

Gilly shook her head. 'No, nothing specific, just that he'd be back in a few days.'

Rowena went to her office, tears of frustration pricking her eyes. She'd been going to ask Clive if she might change her mind and withdraw her resignation and now, almost certainly, it was too late. Jean Brewer had seen all she wanted to see and they had gone up to London to sort out the details and perhaps draw up her contract.

'And I'll bet she drives a hard bargain,' thought Rowena bitterly. 'Awful woman, always laughing that derisive laugh . . . ' And Rowena had a sudden vision of how Jean and Clive had sat at the dinner table, laughing aloud, heads close together. With a jolt she realised that this was the thing that she minded most, Jean's closeness to Clive.

'Which is ridiculous,' she admonished herself aloud. 'You don't even know the man.'

'Except that you do,' pointed out a

small voice inside her. 'You know every inch of his face.'

'Donald's face,' she corrected. 'It's because he's so like Donald and you're missing him. Clive is nothing but a living reminder of Donald.' And Rowena made a conscious effort to visualise Donald — in his chair, the lamplight mellowing his face — but the only picture her mind could provide was the uncompromising face of his brother.

Clive did not return to Chalford for five days, and each day that passed brought Rowena nearer to the time when she must leave. She had made no effort to secure another job; she had not even found herself somewhere to live. Of course her rooms went with the job and she'd have to move out immediately it came to an end. She had decided she would leave her things at her parents' house and take a long holiday before settling down to finding something else to do. After all, she had not been away for more than the odd weekend in all the five years she had been at Chalford, and those were almost all confined to flying visits to her parents in Edinburgh.

'I deserve a holiday,' she told herself, but her heart sank at the thought of it.

★ ★ ★

The night before he came back, Clive telephoned her. Rowena felt her heart jump at the unexpected sound of his voice.

'I'll be back tomorrow, late afternoon,' he told her. 'Perhaps you could join me for dinner? We've a great deal to discuss, and I want to get things sorted out as soon as I can.'

'Yes, of course,' she agreed, but she felt a wave of depression wash over her as she realised what they would be talking about.

Rowena took the next afternoon off. She felt she must have time to prepare herself mentally for what Clive was going to say. She must not let him realise how much she regretted her decision to leave and the emptiness that seemed to stretch ahead of her. It was another perfect summer day and she decided to walk the perimeter of the golf course before getting ready for the evening.

With an easy stride she followed the perimeter path, allowing the sun's warmth to relax her a little. She marvelled at the wealth of wild flowers sheltered in the hedgerows and paused several times to try to identify those unfamiliar to her.

She passed Barry's cottage, sleepy in the sunlight, and as she rounded the garden fence she saw a car parked in the lane beyond. It was a distinctive car, a red Maserati, and she knew at once to whom it belonged; it was often in the members' car park. Even as she wondered what Fay Barber, who owned it, could be doing, the obvious solution came to her.

Rowena strode on angrily. Stupid woman. So much time to do so little that she went in for sordid affairs. Stupid Barry, never able to resist making a conquest even if it could cost him his job if things went wrong. Then Rowena thought of Beryl, the waitress, and wondered if she knew she was only one of Barry's mistresses. And she herself might have been if she had given him any encouragement at all. Rowena smiled grimly. There was something to be said for her dislike of physical contact; she had not been tempted into becoming one of Barry's women.

Despite her discovery of Barry's misdemeanours, Rowena felt better for her walk and went upstairs to dress for dinner feeling a little more relaxed. With her hair washed and loose to her shoulders, her pale yellow silk dress chosen for its elegant simplicity, and her face carefully but lightly made-up, Rowena surveyed herself in the mirror. She knew she was looking good and yet she was full of a shyness and uncertainty alien to her usual confidence. Tonight she would hear the worst, that

Jean Brewer had taken the job, and she herself must appear uncaring as she accepted at last that she must leave.

Clive was waiting for her in the bar and his eyes widened a fraction as he saw her framed in the doorway, her dark hair curling softly to her shoulders and the thin silk of her dress clinging alluringly to her breasts and waist before flaring to fullness over her hips. He stepped forward to meet her and led her to a table by the open window.

'What will you drink?' he asked as he settled her into her chair.

'Gin and tonic, please,' she replied and watched him as he returned to the bar for her drink. He was wearing a charcoal jacket over lighter grey trousers and both seemed to accentuate the returning strength that Rowena had sensed in his body. The lines of pain had gone from his face and it was clear from the way he walked that his leg was troubling him increasingly little.

★ ★ ★

He returned with the drinks. Sitting down beside her, he asked, 'So, has anything happened since I've been away?'

'Nothing in particular. The plans for the Summer Ball have been finalised and the builders intend to make a start on the conservatory towards the end of next week.'

'Yes, well, that's one of the things I want to discuss with you,' said Clive. 'We may hold fire on that project for a month or two.'

Rowena stared at him, consternation in her dark eyes. 'But why? I thought you'd given the idea the go-ahead.'

'I still have in principle,' Clive said, 'but Jean thinks there are more pressing alterations to be done, and it's a question of priorities and cash, you see.'

'Oh,' Rowena said faintly.

'Still,' Clive continued, 'we can talk about that later. Tell me what else has happened since I saw you. There haven't been any more thefts, I hope.'

'None reported.'

'Good. I read through your file on security, it's fairly comprehensive though Jean says that she thinks a house detective even for a short while might be cost effective. Someone to look into the backgrounds of new staff, check up on their movements about the hotel.'

'Sounds like the Gestapo to me,' Rowena said coldly, despite the fact that a house detective had been one of the possibilities she had suggested.

'Oh, I don't know. Just a little checking won't hurt. We must tighten up on security, particularly if there are going to be more members about in future.'

'According to Jean,' Rowena couldn't resist adding. 'Your Jean says too much, if you ask me.'

'But I'm not asking you,' said Clive blandly. 'Shall we go in to dinner?'

Over the meal their conversation was general. No further mention was made of the plans Jean Brewer had for the hotel, and when Rowena remarked that Clive's leg seemed to be much better he replied, 'Yes thank you,' and that topic also was closed.

'We'll have our coffee in the garden flat,' he said when they had finished eating, and, without enquiring if this suited her, he rose from the table and led the way through the hotel. Rowena followed him, grateful in a way that the dreaded discussion would at least take place in private.

'Sit down,' he said when they were in his living-room. 'I'll just put some coffee on.' He disappeared into the kitchen and Rowena looked round with interest at the alterations he had made to the room. A stereo system was set up in one corner with a cabinet of records and tapes beside it. A different picture hung over the mantelpiece, a delicate water colour of lake, hills and mist replacing the rather heavy still life Donald had hung there. Rowena crossed to look at it more closely and noticed that it was signed C. Latimer in one corner. She swung round as Clive came in with the coffee.

'Did you paint that?' she asked.

'No,' replied Clive briefly, 'my mother.'

'It's very beautiful,' said Rowena.

'I like it,' he said. 'Come and have your coffee.'

★   ★   ★

Rowena returned to her chair and accepted the cup he handed her.

'Clive,' she began, and then stopped, unsure of how to go on.

He looked across at her expectantly. 'Yes,' he said encouragingly as she said nothing else.

Rowena drew a deep breath. 'When does Jean take over?' She felt the colour flood her cheeks as he looked at her levelly for a moment, letting the silence lengthen.

'I'm not sure yet,' he replied. 'It all depends . . . '

'On what? I think I'm entitled to have some idea of when I'm needed until.'

'Have you made your own plans?' asked Clive, watching her face intently.

'No — I mean yes — well, nothing's been finalised yet.'

'But of course you've got something lined up?'

'In the pipe-line,' she replied evasively.

'I see,' he said. 'I quite understand you don't want to discuss it with me. It's a pity, though.'

Rowena stared at him. 'What is?'

'The fact that you've got something planned.' He paused, his dark eyes never leaving her face. 'I had hoped you still might change your mind and stay on here.'

'What?' she whispered.

'I had hoped,' Clive repeated gently, 'that you might want to stay on after all.'

'But, but . . . ' stammered Rowena.

'But?' he prompted.

'But what about Jean Brewer?'

'Oh, she couldn't take on the hotel, too,' Clive said firmly. 'I couldn't possibly spare her from Latimer's.'

He waited, still watching Rowena's

face, as his words sank in.

'You couldn't what?' she shrieked, fury bubbling up inside her. 'You mean you never intended . . . ' She spluttered to a halt as she saw that he was laughing.

'Of all the dirty, rotten, underhand tricks!' she exploded, slamming down her coffee cup and leaping to her feet. 'You made me think that that woman . . . '

'I had to, Rowena. There was no other way I could get you to stay. You'd never have swallowed your pride and asked to withdraw your notice. I had to use shock treatment.' The laughter faded from his eyes then and he said gravely, 'I really do need you to stay, you know. Chalford Manor wouldn't be the same without you. Please, Rowena, will you change your mind?'

The anger faded from her face to be replaced by a look of relief as she turned again to face him.

'If you really think we can work

together,' she said quietly, 'I'll give it a go.'

Clive held out his hand to her. 'Then come and sit down and I'll pour us a drink to celebrate.'

'What did you mean about not being able to spare Jean from Latimer's?' she demanded when she was seated again, a brandy in her hand. 'What's Latimer's?'

'It's a small chain of sports shops,' he replied, 'mainly in London.' He paused a moment. 'You know I used to play tennis?'

She nodded.

'Well, when my career in tennis was ruined by a car accident, I opened a sports shop. Now I have several. Jean Brewer helps me run them. I couldn't do without her.'

★   ★   ★

Rowena stared at him. 'You mean, she knew all the time that she wasn't being offered my job?'

Clive's eyes twinkled. 'I'm afraid so,'

he admitted. 'I just told her what things you were most proud of and she made out they would all have to be changed. I really did want you to stay,' he added by way of apology.

'You were fairly unscrupulous,' said Rowena, still nettled that she could be so easily duped.

'I am when it comes to things I want. Remember that, if ever we come into conflict again.'

'What about my swimming pool?' she demanded.

'They're starting next week, aren't they?' he asked innocently.

Rowena shook her head in disbelief. 'I've a feeling I'm going to regret this changed decision,' she said.

'Are you?'

Rowena smiled ruefully. 'No, probably not. I do admit I wasn't looking forward to leaving.'

They finished their drinks and Clive said, 'We'll have to get together in the morning to sort out one or two other matters.'

'Like not employing a house detective to creep round after the staff.'

'Yes,' he agreed with a wolfish grin, 'things like that.' He led her to the door but before he opened it, he said quietly, 'Thank you for changing your mind, Ro.' For a moment he simply held her hand and then he leant forward and gently brushed her lips with his. Rowena stood absolutely still, her wide eyes dark with uncertainty.

'You really are a very beautiful woman,' Clive said softly, putting his arms around her rigid body and bending his head to kiss her again. His lips were firm but gentle; there was nothing of the way he had kissed her on that first morning with anger and force. His arms held her close against him. She could feel the lean line of his body against her own, the gentle pressure of his lips against hers, urging her to part and share the kiss he offered.

For one blissful moment Rowena felt her body relax against his, her mouth admit him, and a feeling of sensuous warmth stir within her as his hands began to caress her. For one moment she felt her body respond as it had to no man since that unwanted advance seven years before. She felt the eagerness rise within her as her arms slipped round him, drawing him close so that her body could mould against his.

And then, suddenly, it began. The blood thundered in her ears and a cold sweat broke out on her forehead. She wrenched her mouth from his, and pushed hard against his chest. For a moment he tried to hold her, his arms tightening to keep her close, but she fought against him violently, struggling to be free. He released her, staring in disbelief at her panic-stricken face.

'Ro, whatever's the matter?' he began.

'Nothing, nothing at all. I just don't like being mauled and manhandled.' As she spoke she struggled with the door handle and jerked the door open. 'So just leave me alone, do you hear, leave me alone.' The note of hysteria in her voice was unmistakable as she disappeared down the corridor without a backward glance, leaving Clive to stare after her in blank astonishment.

6

Once she had gained the sanctuary of her flat, Rowena collapsed into a chair, shivering violently. She was still dry-eyed, but her throat ached as if she had been weeping, and it was some time before she stopped shaking. Then, wearily, she dragged herself into the bedroom and began to undress for bed.

'Clive must think I'm crazy,' she thought miserably. Reluctantly, she let her thoughts wander and came to the conclusion that she had never met anyone like him before. His masculinity assailed her as no other man's had done before. In spite of her latent fear she had felt herself respond; not just when he had kissed her tonight, but before in other ways. She had soon learnt to respect him for his business acumen and quick decisive mind, she had seen the way he coped with pain, relegating it to his lower consciousness, and she admired the courage that enabled him to do so. Gradually he had worked his way into her esteem, despite her initial antagonism and the unfavourable comparisons with Donald. Thoughts of him crept upon her unaware, nudging him into her mind even when she was away from Chalford or occupied with something else. Rowena remembered now the stab of something — had it been jealousy? — when she had seen him tête-à-tête with Jean Brewer at the dinner table.

What she felt for Clive Latimer was not love, she reminded herself, but the fact that she was intensely aware of him as a man was extremely disturbing, and she knew that she must avoid all but the most necessary contact with him. There must be nothing but a formal friendship between them, she decided, for if a more intimate relationship began to develop they might find themselves again in tonight's situation.

Wearily she climbed into bed, determined to maintain her aloofness towards Clive. Even so, she felt a glow of pleasure that she no longer had to leave Chalford Manor. She could continue the work she loved in the place she loved, and that must, as it always had, compensate her for not having a man she loved.

* * *

When she awoke the next morning, it was to hear the bouncing of tennis balls. For one dreadful moment she thought she had overslept, but a glance at her alarm clock assured her it was only a quarter to seven. Intrigued, she got out of bed and peered between her curtains. Below, on one of the tennis courts, was Clive. Dressed in track suit and trainers, he had set up the ball machine and was practising forehands. Rowena watched in awe as shot after shot creamed over the net, clipping the base line in an almost identical spot every time.

The effortless power and grace of the shots were a delight to watch. She knew that Barry was a very good player, that he had followed the tournament circuit for several years when he was younger, but Clive Latimer was in a different class. She watched, entranced, until the ball machine ran out and Clive moved round the court to collect them up. Only then did Rowena notice his limp and remember with an aching heart that Clive would never be able to play really competitive tennis again.

Unaware that anyone was watching, Clive refilled the ball machine and began work on his backhand. Though he moved quickly to take each ball at the optimum moment, Rowena could see now that he lacked the fluidity of movement he would need to reach the top once more, and at thirty-one time was running out. She looked at him critically, taking in the broad power of his shoulders and the length and strength of his legs. He appeared to be a man in his prime, his body tough and lean, without an ounce of extra flesh, a man whose body proclaimed him to be aggressively fit and active except for its one flaw, the weakness which had denied him the chance to achieve the greatness he had striven for.

How can anyone so marvellously athletic and virile be too old? Rowena wondered. He was too old for nothing except the thing he wanted to do most, that was his tragedy, and it made tears prick Rowena's eyes.

Often after that morning Rowena awoke to the sound of tennis balls and allowed herself a few moments' pleasure as she watched Clive working out on the court. She loved to watch him attacking the ball, concentration and determination in every line of his body. Although she was too far away to see his features clearly, Rowena knew what expression would feature on his face.

*   *   *

Neither of them had referred to the incident in the garden flat. Rowena had been a little apprehensive the next day, but Clive said nothing and treated her with a cool courtesy that set the tone of their relationship from then on. He had had to make several trips to London to look after his main business concerns, but he still seemed completely content to leave the day-to-day running of Chalford Manor in her hands.

The conversion of the conservatory was going ahead well and there was much enthusiasm for the project in the club, particularly as it came under the aegis of the hotel and thus was no financial strain on the members.

Clive had, as he promised, arranged all the financial side of the scheme and Rowena had simply to pass on all accounts to him.

'He seems to be an extremely efficient businessman,' she remarked to Barry one evening when they had played tennis and were having their usual shandy on the terrace.

'Pretty hard-headed,' he agreed. 'Didn't take him long to turn his one sports' shop into a chain.'

'I thought you didn't know what he did before he came here,' Rowena challenged.

'I didn't, apart from his tennis, of course. I've been doing a bit of checking.'

'Checking? Why?'

'I like to know who I'm working for,' Barry replied easily.

'Well, I think he's done remarkably well,' said Rowena. 'It can't have been easy after that awful accident. Not only did he have to come to terms with the fact that his tennis career was over, but he had the guts to turn to and make a go of something else.'

'My, my,' said Barry witheringly, 'we are his champion, aren't we? Whatever happened to the arrogant, pompous fellow who caused your resignation not so long ago?'

Rowena laughed ruefully, having forgotten her outburst on the day Clive arrived. 'First impression,' she said, 'I didn't know him then.'

'And you do now?'

'Better than I did. He's got great courage, you know. He hasn't let his tennis go completely. He practises a lot with the ball machine.'

'Won't get him anywhere,' said Barry unpleasantly.

Rowena looked up sharply. 'That's not very kind,' she said.

'He's past it, he knows it, and it's time he accepted it,' replied Barry unrepentantly.

'I do believe you're jealous of him,' she said in surprise.

'Jealous of Latimer?'

'Of his success anyway.'

'I have my own successes, thank you,' snapped Barry, and added with a twisted grin, 'Not quite so public as his, but lucrative in their own way.' Then, before Rowena could question him further, he slipped down off the wall and said, 'I must go, I've got things to see to. By the way, when *does* your notice run out, Ro? You said you were leaving as soon as you could.'

Rowena coloured at his question and said uneasily, 'I — er — well, I've withdrawn my notice. I'm staying on.'

'Are you now?' Barry looked at her speculatively. 'I see.'

'What do you see?' she demanded hotly.

'Everything,' said Barry enigmatically. 'Night.' And he left her glowering after him, feeling he had scored off her in some way.

★   ★   ★

Clive supposedly had gone up to London for a couple of days, and so when he appeared in Rowena's office next afternoon she was surprised to see him.

'You're back early,' she said. 'I thought you were away until tomorrow.'

'I finished sooner than I thought and

so I made an appointment with Kelland — it's in half-an-hour. I just wanted to check the final arrangements for the Midsummer Ball with you.'

'Yes, of course. It's next Friday, the 21st June. We've a marquee on the lawn with a steel band, a disco in the terrace room, buffet set out in the dining-room. There's an awning from the terrace to the marquee just in case it's wet with matting underfoot, of course, and Grover is putting up the usual coloured lights on the terrace and in the top garden.'

'Hmm,' grunted Clive. 'Timing?'

'Nine for nine-thirty, carriages at two.'

'Right. We'll have to be there from the start, so I'll collect you from your flat at a quarter to nine.'

Rowena stared at him. 'I beg your pardon?'

'Unless you'd rather come over to the garden flat for a drink first.'

'No, thank you.' She spoke too vehemently and Clive gave a tight smile.

'I thought not. But I assume you do attend the ball.'

'Of course, we always . . . '

'We. You and Donald. You and the proprietor. You and me.'

'But I can't . . . ' Rowena began again.

'Why not? Are you going with someone else?'

'No.'

'Well, then, all the arrangements are made, the social committee runs the ball — it's not your problem, is it?'

'Not strictly, but even so I do like to keep an eye on things.'

'So do I,' said Clive smoothly, 'and it's time I met the members here. What better chance will I get, particularly with you there to make the introductions?'

Rowena felt trapped. Part of her longed to accept Clive's suggestion, because as always when he was near her she felt his magnetism drawing her closer. And yet this was the very reason she should say no. The attraction she felt was in itself a danger because of the inevitable rejection she knew would follow.

However, Clive gave her no chance to refuse, saying briskly: 'I'm afraid you'll have to regard it as part of your job. You can always put in for overtime.'

'That won't be necessary.' Rowena bristled, her original antagonism re-appearing as she outfaced his arrogant stare.

'Suit yourself,' he replied with a shrug. 'Now, just give me the latest on the pool. I won't have time to go and look today, and I'm off to London again tomorrow.'

Rowena relaxed a little as she told Clive how far the pool contractors had got. Warming to her subject, she added, 'It really is going to look marvellous when it's finished.'

For a moment Clive's coolness disappeared and he smiled. 'Great,' he said. 'You can show it all to me at the weekend. I won't go and look at it without you.' He crossed to the door.

'See you on Friday evening, Rowena. I'll be up to fetch you at quarter to nine.' And with that he disappeared, leaving Rowena to brood on his arrogance.

She was not left alone for long, however, for within minutes of Clive's departure Gilly appeared, looking troubled.

'Sorry, Rowena,' she said, 'but it's happened again. Some money's gone missing from a guest's room.'

It took the rest of the afternoon to deal with the guest, Mr. Pearman, who had left his wallet in his bedside drawer while playing tennis with Barry, and the police, whom he demanded should be sent for.

When at last statements had been taken and the police had gone, Rowena borrowed the hotel register and checked guests' names and dates as the detectives had asked her to do. It did not take long to establish that on the four or five occasions when money had vanished, the entire guest list had been different. No guest had been staying in the hotel on more than one occasion when things had been stolen.

'Which means,' Rowena decided, 'that either we've got a series of isolated thefts, a thief who comes in occasionally from the outside, or else it's one of the staff. Whichever, it will get the place a bad name and it must be stopped.'

She thought hard and long about the matter and decided she really must pin Clive down to some sort of security check. If it meant a house detective, after all, then that was the price they must pay.

★   ★   ★

Friday June 21st was an extremely busy day for Chalford, but Rowena was thankfully not called upon to do much. The country club's social committee always ran the Midsummer Ball, and this year was no exception. It was they who had discussed menus with Danny, arranged flowers, hired the marquee, helped Grover, the groundsman, rig the coloured lights, booked the band and the disco.

Rowena began her day by chivvying the pool contractors and checking the autumn programme before it went to the printers. Occasionally, however, her hands would fall idly to her desk and she would find herself thinking about the evening ahead. By lunchtime she could no longer concentrate on her work.

'This is ridiculous,' she said aloud. 'I'm going out.' She went down to reception and said to Gilly, 'I'll be out for the rest of the day.'

Gilly stared at her. 'But it's the Midsummer Ball,' she gasped.

'I'm well aware it's the Midsummer Ball,' Rowena replied with some asperity. 'I shall be back for that, but just now I'm going out. The social committee can run this ball standing on their heads. They won't even know I'm not here.'

Leaving Gilly staring dumbfounded

after her, Rowena swept out of the hall, collected her car from its garage and drove to Bath where she decided on impulse to treat herself to a slap-up lunch.

When she reached the city, however, she was not hungry and decided to window shop a while before finding somewhere to eat. She passed a pleasant hour wandering in the little lanes and arcades that made up the pedestrian precinct and just as she turned at last towards a little wine bar she knew, Rowena caught sight of something that made her catch her breath. On the single model in the window of a boutique opposite was a long evening dress. Its pale green chiffon clung seductively to the model's straight, stiff body, the bodice cut low across the bosom, the skirt falling in soft folds to the floor. For a long moment Rowena stared at it and then, ignoring the alarming figure on the discreet price tag, went into the shop.

It was darker inside, and Rowena's

eyes took time to adjust. Then, as the one assistant was clearly busy at the cash desk with a customer, she began to look along the racks until it was her turn.

'One hundred and seventy-five pounds, please, madam,' Rowena heard the shop girl say. Glancing over the dress rail she saw the customer count out the money in ten-and five-pound notes. Then she realised with a jolt who the customer was, and could hardly believe her eyes. Surely that was Beryl, the waitress, paying one hundred and seventy-five pounds for a dress.

Instinctively, Rowena drew back behind the rack of clothes and turned away from the counter so that Beryl should not see her. She remained apparently absorbed in the dresses on the rail behind her until she heard the assistant bidding her customer goodbye and the doorbell jingling as she left. Her mind was turning somersaults. It had been Beryl, hadn't it? Rowena was almost certain her eyes had not deceived her, but where on earth had Beryl got money like that to spend? Had Barry given it to her or was Beryl adding to her income in some other way? Was Beryl the thief? Had it really been she?

'Can I help you?' The assistant broke in on her thoughts.

'Oh, yes. The dress in the window,' she answered. 'I'd like to try it on, please.'

The assistant fetched the dress and Rowena set aside all thoughts of Beryl as she felt the softness of the material in her hands. She retired to a fitting-room then emerged to stand before the full-length mirror.

She could hardly believe that she was looking at herself. The woman who gazed back at her from the looking-glass seemed like a stranger, tall, elegant and sophisticated. The clinging material emphasised the narrowness of her waist and the swell of her hips before sweeping gracefully to the floor. The low neckline revealed the sensuous curve of her breasts and two bootlace straps on each shoulder maintained the delicacy of the creation while supporting a deep vee-shaped line to the back of the dress.

Rowena had never worn a gown like it. Feeling it might give her the confidence she needed to face the evening ahead, she nodded briefly and retired once more to the fitting-room. The assistant smiled at the drawn curtain. From the moment madam had appeared wearing the dress she had known she had a sale.

Rowena missed lunch altogether. With the dress carefully packed into a box, she spent the rest of the afternoon looking for evening shoes and replenishing her stock of make-up.

★　★　★

As the hands of the clock approached a quarter to nine, she felt decidedly fluttery. She awaited Clive's arrival in a state of confusion. Wearing the magnificent willow-green gown, her hair swept up on her head, her gold drop earrings dancing and a gold chain necklace about her throat, she knew with sudden certainty that tonight she was beautiful. She smiled tremulously at her reflection and felt tears well in her eyes. She had never dressed like this for Donald but she had never felt like this for him — or any man.

In her heart she ached for Clive to find her as attractive as she found him; for him to hold her once more in his arms and once more call forth the passion within her. In her mind she was afraid. Suppose her reaction was the same? No man would take rejection twice, especially if she had appeared to encourage him first. He would dismiss her as a common flirt, if not worse.

There was a knock at the door and Rowena paused a moment before she drew in a deep breath and answered it.

Clive stood on the threshold, incredibly good-looking in his well-cut dinner jacket and immaculate white shirt. His dark eyes widened in admiration and perhaps something else as he saw Rowena waiting for him, an elusive smile hovering on her lips. He took a step forward and Rowena drew aside to let him in. He walked into her living-room, looking around him. He had not been in to her apartment before, there had been no reason for him to and Rowena had not invited him. Now, as she expected him to make some comment about her appearance, he simply said, 'This is a lovely room, Rowena. It suits you so well.'

She felt a stab of disappointment. Clearly Clive did not notice her in the way she had hoped. He was not even looking at her but standing at the window looking down on the floodlit driveway as if to see if any guests were arriving. Then he turned back.

'Ready?' he asked lightly.

'Of course,' she replied, picking up the evening bag she had bought to match her evening shoes. 'Let's go down and face the music.'

Clive led her to the door and then

suddenly took her hand in his. 'You look stunning,' he murmured, and as the colour flooded her cheeks he added with a grin, 'Even more so when you blush.' Though he released her at once Rowena could feel the warmth of his hand on hers long after they had descended to the hall ready to greet the guests as they arrived.

She had a particularly good memory for names and as each member or group of members arrived she introduced them to Clive.

★ ★ ★

The Midsummer Ball was *the* social event locally and every lady who arrived had clearly dressed to outshine her friends and rivals. Rowena could only marvel at the magnificent variety of evening gowns; the style and elegance of some, the daring and frivolity of others. Family jewels had been reclaimed from the bank and everywhere diamonds sparkled as they caught the light, warm and milky pearls clung to throats and wrists, and there was the occasional flash of blue fire from a sapphire ring or pendant.

'Goodness knows what this lot is worth,' Clive murmured to Rowena as Mrs. Morton-Harvey bore down on them. She wore a low-necked designer gown of plain black silk and a diamond choker, brilliant in the lamplight. Diamond sparks flew from the matching bracelet on her wrist and the pendant earrings that danced as she turned her head. With her was her husband, Charles, suave and urbane, and two other couples, the Millers and the Barbers. Jane Miller and Fay Barber, in a determined effort not to be outdone, were clearly wearing their finest gems.

'Unless of course they're paste,' Clive muttered as an afterthought at which Rowena was hard-put to keep from laughing aloud. She managed to introduce the group to Clive without disgracing herself, however, and felt a sudden surge of happiness as she saw Clive's eyes twinkling at her, sharing their joke, while apparently attending to something Mrs. Morton-Harvey was saying before the group moved off to shed their fur coats and drift out to the marquee.

Despite the warmth of the evening most of the women arrived either carrying or wearing furs, and these were left under the watchful eye of Amy, doing duty as a cloakroom attendant. The men, immaculate in their dinner jackets and fancy evening shirts, were the perfect foil for the butterfly beauty of their women.

It was clear Clive was used to mixing with people he did not know, for he was never at a loss for a word or an answer as the members and their guests streamed in. Before long the hotel's reception rooms were crowded and there was a general hubbub of laughter, chatter and general good humour. Rowena began to circulate amongst the groups, talking to friends, listening to the occasional grouse about something within the club, but every time she glanced up she found that Clive was not far away, his eyes resting upon her in a strangely proprietorial manner. As before she felt confused as she feared the outcome of the evening.

Barry arrived alone, and as soon as he saw her crossed to Rowena's side.

'Hi,' he said, kissing her lightly on the cheek. 'You look ravishing. Shall I get you a drink?'

Rowena smiled at him, fighting her instinctive recoil as she felt his lips on her face.

'No thanks, Barry, I've got one somewhere. I put it down over there when I was introducing someone to Clive.' She retrieved her glass, holding it before her like a shield. She did not like Barry's mood; he seemed belligerent. Clearly, although he was not drunk, he had been drinking and it made her uneasy.

'The steel band have started to play in the marquee,' he said. 'I can hear them. Shall we go and look? People may be dancing. Let's go and dance.'

'I can't,' she answered. 'I'm sorry, but I said I'd stay with Clive and introduce him to the members as they arrived. They're not all here yet.'

Barry glanced across at Clive. 'Looks as if he's doing all right on his own,' he said sourly. 'Still, he's the boss. Her master's voice and all that. If you've no time for me, I'll go and dance with one of my favourite pupils.'

He raised his hand in mock salute and wandered over to the group where the Morton-Harveys were standing chatting with the Barbers. Rowena remembered the red Maserati parked outside Barry's cottage and for a moment was filled with intense misgivings.

'You look worried.' Clive was suddenly at her elbow. 'What's that fool Barry Short been saying?'

★   ★   ★

Rowena gave herself a mental shake and forced a smile. 'Nothing. I just hope he behaves himself, that's all.'

'He will,' Clive said with grim confidence, 'or he'll be out on his ear. Come on, let's have another drink before we eat.'

Danny had surpassed himself, and though Clive and Rowena were among the last to pass along the buffet table there was still a vast selection of foods to choose from. Several of the waitresses were ensconced behind the long white-clad tables serving food to the guests. Beryl was there, neat in her black uniform dress and crisp white apron and cap. Rowena watched her for a moment, dispensing slices of succulent pink salmon, and wondered again. Had it really been her she had seen in the boutique in Bath? She had been certain at the time, but surely she must have been here, helping with the buffet? It was something she must remember to check out.

By the time they had finished eating, most people were dancing. The disco in the terrace room attracted many of the younger members. Glancing in at the door Rowena could see, amid the flashing lights and gyrating bodies, that Barry was there, dancing energetically with three girls at once. It made her smile. Typical Barry. Never happy unless surrounded by admiring females.

'Come and dance to the steel band.' Clive was at her elbow again. Smiling up at him, she placed her hand in his extended one and allowed herself to be led through to the marquee. The dance floor was crowded, everyone swaying gently to the mellifluous tones of a soft Jamaican calypso. As they joined the throng, Clive slipped an arm around Rowena's waist and they moved in unison to the sensuous rhythm.

His touch was light on her back, and Rowena had long since come to terms with a man holding her politely on a dance floor; after all, she had only to move for the hold to be broken. If she did feel the man's arms beginning to tighten, to draw her closer than she liked, she would smilingly disengage herself, pleading the heat or the need for a drink. With Clive, however, she felt no need of these subterfuges for he made no effort to draw her to him and she danced in the circle of his arm without constraint.

At the end of the dance the music changed and Rowena was claimed by one of the members, Paul Sheraton, while Clive was carried off by Paul's wife. There was no question of close dancing to the next exuberant tune which the band played and they all danced with uninhibited pleasure as the rhythm claimed their bodies and minds. From then on Rowena never lacked a partner, and in the general jollity she only caught occasional glimpses of Clive dancing with one after another of the ladies who were vying for his attention.

When at last the band took pity on them all and slipped quietly into more romantic mood, Rowena thanked her last partner and moved off the dance floor. She had hoped Clive would come and find her again, but she saw him locked in the arms of Fay Barber. With a sharp stab of disappointment, she turned to go back into the hotel.

'Oh, no you don't,' Barry was at her side, his hand grasping her waist firmly. 'Come and have a dance. I haven't been able to get near you so far and you won't escape me now.'

'I haven't been trying to escape you,' Rowena protested, laughing, trying to pull free of his grip. But Barry did not let go, simply stepped on to the dance floor, saying, 'Good. Let's dance.'

* * *

He pulled her into his arms, linking his hands behind her back to crush her closely against him. Rowena put both hands against his chest to push him away but his hold did not relax but rather increased so that her face was pressed against his shoulder and she felt smothered. As one arm held her firmly against him, Barry allowed his other hand to smooth the silky skin of Rowena's back, revealed by the plunging backline of her gown.

'Barry, for goodness' sake,' she muttered.

'What's the matter?' he said, grinning down at her. 'Don't you like it?'

'No, I don't! If you want to dance, fine, but I dislike being mauled in public.'

'How about in private, Ro? Would that be better? I've longed to have you to myself for an evening. Can't you feel how much I want you?' Both arms tightened again and he pressed her against him so that she could feel his arousal. At the same time she felt his lips on her neck kissing the sensitive hollow beneath her ear. The familiar thundering began in her ears. She must break free.

'Barry, for heaven's sake, stop it,' she rebuked him and with a sudden surge of strength she jerked herself free and ran from the dance floor.

Barry, white with rage at being left

flat, strode quickly after her. He caught up with her on the terrace, grabbed her by the wrist and dragged her into the shadows beyond the glow of the fairy lights.

'Don't you dare storm away from me like that,' he raged. 'If I want to kiss you, I'll damn well kiss you. It's time somebody did.'

Holding her fiercely against him, he lowered his head and began to kiss her with a violence that bruised her lips. Rowena tried to twist away, pummelling him with her fists, but her struggles only increased his determination.

She fought down the rising panic, the roaring in her head which accompanied it, and went completely limp. As she did so, Barry raised his head and gave a short derisive laugh.

'Your middle-aged Donald didn't ever kiss you like that, did he?' he sneered. 'I bet you're still a virgin.' He made the word an insult. 'You don't even like being kissed.'

'Just because I don't fling myself into

your arms, or your bed, like Fay Barber and that little fool Beryl, doesn't mean I don't like men. It means I don't like *you*, that's all.'

'I expect it's dear Clive you're after,' Barry jeered. 'You lost the club because Donald didn't come up to scratch, and the only way you'll get your hands on it now is to marry Clive — if you can get him. What a scheming little bitch you are, a scheming frigid little bitch,' he amended, and at last released her. 'At least Beryl has something to offer — a warm responsive body. Making love to you would be a penance not a pleasure. Poor Clive, I pity him.'

'When I want your pity, Short, I'll ask for it,' Clive's voice came icily from the darkness. 'You may leave at the end of the week. In the meantime, I don't expect to see you in the club house or hotel again — starting now.'

'You can't do that,' said Barry, spinning round to confront Clive. 'I've got a contract until the end of September.'

'I've just terminated it.'

'It will cost you a great deal of money,' Barry said angrily.

'It'll be cheap at the price,' replied Clive coolly. 'You may leave here now and be out of the cottage in seven days.'

Barry stared at Clive dumbfounded for a moment and then turned back to Rowena. But she was no longer there. The moment she had heard Clive speak, and realised that he had overheard part, if not all, of her row with Barry, she felt a wave of humiliation sweep over her.

Unable to face either man again she left them to their dispute and slipped away. As far as she was concerned, the ball was over. She crept upstairs to the privacy of her room, where at last she found relief in tears.

7

Her reprieve was over, Rowena knew that now. It would be impossible for her to remain at Chalford Manor. As she relived her exchange with Barry, she realised that however much or little Clive had overheard it would be too much. She could not bear to hear that he had caught any of it, and with this came another realisation — the knowledge of just how important Clive had become to her. At last she faced what perhaps she had known for some time but had refused to acknowledge. She had fallen in love with Clive. She loved him as she had never loved anyone. The warm affection she had felt for his brother paled into insignificance beside the love she felt for Clive. But it was a love without a future for if she had been unable to bring herself to marry Donald, knowing she could not offer the final commitment of herself, body and soul, how much less could she marry Clive, loving him as she did, without being able to give herself completely.

So she would resign once more and this time she would not be persuaded to withdraw that resignation, whatever pressure Clive exerted. She knew him better now than when he had introduced Jean Brewer, and she knew that he would never change the essence of Chalford Manor. He would find another manager who would carry on as she, Rowena, had done, and little would change.

Determined to act while the mood of resolution was upon her, Rowena found paper and an envelope and wrote her letter of resignation. She read it through once, sealed it, and addressed it to Clive ready to leave it on his desk in the morning. Weary, empty, but strangely calm, she at last sought her bed and the oblivion of sleep.

Her appearance downstairs next morning was greeted with relief by Gilly.

'Oh, Rowena, thank goodness. Mrs. Morton-Harvey's been on the phone already and there's no sign of the coat.'

'Coat, what coat?' asked Rowena, puzzled.

'Mrs. Morton-Harvey's. Her fur. It was taken last night. She says it was stolen, but we've pointed out that it may well have been taken in error.'

'Much more likely, I should think,' said Rowena calmly. 'Does Mr. Latimer know about this?'

'Yes, he was here last night when the coat was missed. It was he who suggested Mrs. Morton-Harvey rang this morning to see if it had been returned.'

'Then next time she rings, I should put her straight through to Mr. Latimer.'

'I can't,' wailed Gilly. 'He's left already.'

'Left?' Rowena's heart sank. 'Where's he gone, did he say?'

'He said he was going to London for a few days. It's Wimbledon fortnight, isn't it? He's left you a note.' Gilly passed Rowena a sealed envelope from behind the desk and she retired to her office to read it. It was brief and to the point.

'*Dear Rowena,*

I shall be in London most of this week and next for Wimbledon. You can contact me at the above number in an emergency, but if not I'll see you this coming Friday — I've a meeting with Kelland and I want to check Short has vacated the cottage. If you have any trouble with him, contact me at once. Perhaps you'd like a day at Wimbledon next week? I suggest Friday for the men's semi-finals. Keep it free.
Clive.'

★ ★ ★

Rowena stared at the letter and then glanced at her resignation in its sealed envelope. How lovely a day at Wimbledon would be, she thought. Surely it wouldn't hurt to accept this last invitation?

'It'll give you something to remember,' a voice whispered inside her, 'a last day with Clive.'

'I can't,' she said aloud. 'It's not fair.'

'It wouldn't hurt,' whispered her inner voice, 'just one day.'

'I'll see,' Rowena told herself, but before going out of her office she paused and drew a line through her diary for Friday week. No appointments.

Mrs. Morton-Harvey was soon on the telephone again, and Rowena had great difficulty in calming her down.

'I've reported the matter to the police,' Mrs. Morton-Harvey said. 'They'll be up to see you. I want all the servants' quarters searched, and all the rooms. You've got a thief there, Rowena, and I want my coat.'

'I hardly think a thief would keep a stolen coat in his or her bedroom,' she pointed out reasonably. 'I can't see that a search is likely to turn up much.'

'You needn't think we'll let the matter rest,' the woman went on relentlessly. 'We shall get a search warrant if necessary. My husband is a personal friend of the chief constable's.'

'I'm sure that won't be necessary,' soothed Rowena. 'I'll talk to the police when they come and we'll try and sort something out. But, do remember, with so many people here last night it could easily have been someone walking in off the street.'

'It was in your care; I left it in an attended cloakroom. I shall sue you for gross negligence if that coat is not recovered.' Mrs. Morton-Harvey slammed down the receiver and Rowena replaced hers thoughtfully. The woman had a point, she supposed. Amy should have been on duty all evening.

Rowena sent for the chamber maid.

'I told Mr. Latimer last night — I don't know anything about it. I didn't give no one a coat without them giving me a ticket. They were all numbered.'

'I see,' said Rowena gently, 'and what

happened when Mrs. Morton-Harvey gave you her ticket?'

'I looked on the rack but the coat wasn't there.'

'And you checked every other coat in case you'd muddled the tickets when you handed them out?'

Amy was close to tears and blinking furiously. 'Yes,' she sniffed. 'I looked everywhere, and there wasn't no other coat left after, to show that someone took the wrong one. But I didn't take it, Miss Winston — I didn't take Mrs. Morton-Harvey's coat!'

'No, I'm sure you didn't, Amy,' said Rowena soothingly. 'No one thinks you did.'

'Mrs. Morton-Harvey thinks I did.'

'I'm sure she doesn't.'

'Yes, she does,' said Amy stubbornly. 'She said so. She said I must have given it to someone or taken it myself.'

'I don't expect she meant it,' Rowena said. 'I expect she was upset at the time.'

'That's what Mr. Latimer said,' cried

Amy, 'but she said she was going to call the police and I'd be arrested.'

'Well, you won't,' said Rowena firmly. 'Now don't worry, I'll deal with the police if and when they arrive. She has to report the disappearance or her insurance company won't pay the claim. Did you leave the coakroom at any time during the evening?'

Amy shook her head vigorously.

'Are you sure, Amy? Even just for a moment could be important.'

'Well, I did go to the toilet a couple of times, but I was very quick.'

'I'm sure you were, but it might have given the thief the chance he needed just to grab a coat and run.'

★   ★   ★

On her own once more, Rowena sat lost in thought. Clearly the fur had been stolen; if it had been taken in error another must have been left behind. Undoubtedly the police would be coming before very long, and Rowena dreaded an official room search, particularly as most of the staff had been at the club for several years and she considered them above suspicion. It was far more likely that a professional thief had heard of the ball, knew that there might be pickings and had infiltrated, dressed in evening dress probably, to see what he could take. There were the hotel guests, too, of course; any of them could have slipped in and removed the coat. The police would have to produce search warrants to search their rooms.

She wondered if any had checked out already; she must find out. She also wondered if she should try and contact Clive, but soon decided against that. He already knew that the coat was missing but it had not detained him; he had made no mention of it in his note so obviously he considered her quite capable of dealing with the situation. So she was, she thought with determination. And having made her decision as to what she was going to do, she set out to implement it at once.

At the reception desk she asked Gilly if anyone had checked out today.

Gilly shook her head. 'And no one's due to either,' she said. 'The guests are mostly weekenders and are here till tomorrow afternoon.'

'Right,' said Rowena. 'I'll mind the shop. I want you to go and ask all the living-in staff to come to my office, then come back and take over from me here.'

Gilly did as Rowena asked and ten minutes later they were all assembled in the office. Rowena explained what had happened.

'Now the problem is, Mrs. Morton-Harvey wants the whole place searched. Rather than have the police tramping through unnecessarily, I wondered if we could search the staff rooms ourselves. I must emphasise I'm not expecting to find anything, but once we are all eliminated — and my flat will be searched, too — then we shall have only the guests to worry about.'

There were murmurs of agreement

and Rowena went on, 'I suggest Danny and I search together, then either of us will be an independent witness if anything is found.' She looked around the staff carefully. 'We are all here, aren't we?'

'All except Beryl,' said Danny. 'It's her day off and she's already gone out.'

'I see.' Rowena thought for a moment. 'What shall we do about her room?'

Danny shrugged. 'Don't suppose she'd mind,' he said. 'She'd probably rather we looked than the police did.'

Again there was a general murmur of agreement and Rowena said, 'Right then, let's try and get this done before the police arrive. Any of you may, of course, stay in your rooms while they're being searched.'

* * *

The search did not take long and as Rowena had expected they found nothing. Every room, including her own flatlet, was thoroughly searched and at last there was only Beryl's room left. The rest of the living-in staff had returned to their work and it was only Danny and Rowena who went into the room which Rowena unlocked with a pass key. A quick look in the wardrobe and drawers showed there was no fur coat hidden anywhere and they were about to leave again when Danny said, 'There's a suitcase under the bed. Perhaps we ought to look in there.'

They dragged it out, but when they tried to open it they found it was locked. Danny looked across it at Rowena.

'What do we do?' he asked.

Rowena shrugged. 'We can't break it open,' she said.

'I suppose not,' he agreed reluctantly. 'But it's got something in it. It's too heavy to be empty.' He shook the case. It did not rattle but something moved inside.

They were still kneeling together on the floor, looking at the locked case, when Gilly appeared.

'The police are here,' she said. 'They want to speak to you, Rowena.'

She got up. 'Fine,' she said. 'I'll come down.'

'What do we do about this?' asked Danny, pointing to the suitcase.

'Bring it with us and see what the police say.'

Gilly had shown the two policemen, Sergeant Doller and Constable Prout, into the office. Rowena and Danny joined them there with Beryl's suitcase.

Rowena quickly explained the situation to them.

'It should be opened in Beryl Hacker's presence,' said Sergeant Doller. 'Is she in the hotel?'

'I don't think so,' said Rowena. 'It's her day off.'

At that moment Danny, who had been standing by the window, said, 'There she is, just coming up the drive.'

'Perhaps you'd be good enough to ask her to step in here for a few moments, sir,' said Sergeant Doller.

He returned moments later with an angry Beryl who strode into the office, declaring: 'It's my day off, Miss Winston. I won't be sent for . . . ' But the words died on her lips when she saw her suitcase on the floor and two policemen in the room.

'Miss Hacker?' said Sergeant Doller.

'Yes, what do *you* want?'

'Is this your suitcase, Miss Hacker?'

'No,' said Beryl.

'It was found in your bedroom, Miss Hacker.'

'It's not mine.'

'If it's not yours, Miss Hacker, then you can have no objection to our opening it, can you?' said the sergeant smoothly. 'Normally, Miss Winston,' he went on, turning to Rowena, 'we'd need the consent of the owner. But as we have no idea who the owner is, I think we'd better force the case open in the hope we can identify him or her from its contents.'

Beryl turned sharply to look at the doorway but Constable Prout was standing there watching the proceedings and there was no escape that way.

With the aid of the steel-bladed paper knife on Rowena's desk the sergeant levered open the catches of the case and looked inside. There was no fur coat, but the case was certainly not empty. There were a few clothes, a bag bearing the name of the boutique in Bath, and underneath them several purses and wallets, some trinkets of jewellery, and three large brown envelopes with names scrawled in their corners.

★   ★   ★

The sergeant lifted out each wallet and looked inside. There was no money in any of them, but one contained a check book for the account of a Mr. H. Wolfe, and another had several credit cards in the name of Mr. D. Harland. The sergeant glanced across at Beryl who stood ashen-faced, watching him. Without a word he picked up the three envelopes and read out the names. 'Celia Morton-Harvey, Angela Thomas, Fay Barber. Do these names mean anything to anyone here?'

Beryl remained mute but Rowena said: 'Yes, sergeant. They're all members of this club.'

'What is in these envelopes?' Sergeant Doller asked Beryl.

'How should I know?' she said. 'It's not my suitcase.'

The sergeant sighed and upended one of the envelopes on to the desk.

'Good grief,' breathed Rowena as she saw the contents. 'I don't believe it.'

Sergeant Doller picked up one of the large glossy photographs that had tumbled on to the desk.

'Do you know these people?' he asked Rowena, holding up the picture by its corners but not allowing her to touch it.

She gulped and nodded. The photograph was an extremely clear picture of Celia Morton-Harvey with Barry Short. They were not playing tennis.

'Is it the person named on the envelope?'

Rowena nodded again.

Extremely delicately, still holding the prints by the corners, the sergeant replaced them in the envelope. Then he opened each of the others in turn and similar pictures of Barry with Angela Thomas and Barry with Fay Barber were revealed.

'Who is this man?' Sergeant Doller asked.

'Barry Short, our tennis coach.'

'I wonder who took these?' mused the sergeant, and then glanced sharply at Beryl. 'Any idea, Miss Hacker?'

Beryl shook her head but her defiance had seeped away and she burst into tears.

'He made me,' she wept. 'He made me take them. He said they were all silly rich bitches with nothing to do. They could afford to pay and then we could get married. He made me keep the pictures in case his place was searched.'

'Perhaps, Miss Winston,' said the sergeant, 'you'd be kind enough to lend us your office for a little while.'

'Certainly,' she replied. 'Come on, Danny.'

'You both realise, of course, that no mention of any of this is to go any further,' the policeman reminded them, and Rowena and Danny assured him that they did.

'Perhaps, Miss Winston, you'd be kind enough to give the three ladies concerned a ring and ask them to come over as soon as possible. There's no need for long explanations. I'll deal with them when they get here.'

Danny and Rowena left the still snivelling Beryl and the two policemen and went back downstairs, Danny reluctantly to the kitchen and Rowena to make the telephone calls.

★ ★ ★

Celia Morton-Harvey arrived before the other two and swept up to the reception desk, demanding in ringing tones whether anything had been discovered about her coat.

Rowena greeted her politely and said that the police were indeed there and were waiting to speak to her.

'I'll just tell them you've arrived,' she said. 'I won't be one moment.'

The rest of the morning had a nightmare quality about it. Celia Morton-Harvey strode into her meeting with the police, full of righteous indignation, and emerged later, red-eyed and deathly pale. By this time Angela Thomas had arrived and she in turn was interviewed by the police. Rowena looked at the shaken Mrs. Morton-Harvey and felt suddenly sorry for her.

'Can I get you a drink?' she asked softly. 'If you like you can sit upstairs in my flat until you're more composed, or I could ring your husband and ask him to come and fetch you.'

'No,' cried Celia. 'I can't face Charles yet.' She stared across at Rowena and said dully, 'You know, don't you?'

Rowena nodded. 'It's a dreadful thing to happen,' she said.

'It's my own fault,' Celia replied bleakly. 'I thought it'd be a bit of fun. It was the first couple of times, and then the pictures arrived. He threatened to send them to my husband if I didn't pay what he asked.'

'Is that when you decided to resign?' asked Rowena, light suddenly dawning.

Celia nodded. 'But when Barry found out, he said if I didn't withdraw my resignation he'd send the photos to Charles anyway.'

'I see.'

'He must have done the same to Angela Thomas,' Rowena thought, which would account for her resignation and its sudden withdrawal.

'I paid once,' Celia went on bitterly, 'but he kept on asking for more. I couldn't get the money without telling Charles. I didn't know what to do.' Now she had begun to talk, Celia Morton-Harvey seemed unable to stop.

'In the end I decided I'd have to sell something, but I was afraid any of my jewellery would soon be missed. Then I thought of my fur coat.'

'Your coat,' repeated Rowena puzzled. 'You mean you stole your own fur coat?'

Celia nodded miserably.

'Where is it now?' Rowena demanded angrily, thinking of all the trouble this woman had caused.

'In my golf locker. I thought if I took it and then said it had been stolen, the insurance would replace it and I could sell it privately to pay off Barry.'

'Until he asked for more again,' snapped Rowena.

'But what else could I do?' cried Celia in despair. 'It could ruin my husband if it came out. He's a barrister, you know, hoping to take silk.'

'It'll come out now anyway, I suppose,' said Rowena. 'I assume that you'll press charges.'

'I don't think it's in my hands,' said Celia miserably. 'Anyway, I gather I'm not the only one.'

Rowena refused to be drawn on that but said, 'Come and sit in the bar. I'll get you a drink and when you've calmed down a little I should go home and tell your husband everything.'

'I can't,' wailed Celia. 'I can't face Charles.'

'You're going to have to,' said Rowena firmly, 'and I'm sure he'd rather hear about it from you than from the police.'

She was just settling Celia in the bar with a large brandy when she heard Barry's voice in reception, raised and demanding. Celia gave a little squeal and Rowena rounded on her.

'Shut up,' she hissed. 'He doesn't know he's caught yet. Do you want him to make a run for it?'

Celia shook her head dumbly and Rowena went casually out to reception.

'I want to see Latimer,' Barry was saying to Gilly. 'You tell him I'm here — with my contract.'

'All right, Gilly, I'll see to Barry,' said Rowena. 'Don't make a scene here,' she went on. 'Clive's not here today. Why don't you come up to my office and you can tell me what you want him for.'

'I want to talk to the organ-grinder not the monkey,' snapped Barry rudely.

'Clive is in London,' said Rowena. 'Come on, come up to my office and we'll see what we can sort out. Bring that with you,' she added, nodding towards the terms of employment he had been waving in the air.

★ ★ ★

Barry followed her upstairs and when she reached her office door she turned the handle and then stood aside for him to pass in front of her. As he stepped over the threshold he suddenly realised the office was occupied. In an instant he took in the photographs spread out on the desk. Afraid he'd escape, Rowena gave him a sharp unexpected push which made him stumble into the room, then she stepped in behind him and closed the door, saying as she did so, 'This is Barry Short.'

There was no denial he could make in the face of the evidence; Angela Thomas had even produced the letter he had sent threatening to expose her to her husband if she made a scene and left Chalford Manor. By the time Fay Barber appeared, her evidence was purely corroborative.

Barry and Beryl were both taken off in the second police car which had appeared at Sergeant Doller's request. Beryl had been removed from Rowena's office by the time Barry arrived. When they met in the hall, each escorted by a policeman, Beryl still snivelling, Barry just glanced at her contemptuously.

'Silly fool,' he remarked. 'If you'd kept your greedy little hands to yourself we wouldn't be in this mess.'

Beryl burst into tears again and both were led out to the waiting car. Sergeant Doller drove the three women involved down to the police station and Rowena collapsed into a chair, feeling completely drained. Guests were going into the dining-room for lunch and there was a speculative buzz of conversation amongst those who had seen the uniformed police take Beryl and Barry away. Glancing at the clock, Rowena saw that the hands stood at 12.45. The whole unpleasant episode had taken less than three hours, but to her the morning had seemed an eternity.

As she sat thinking, re-living the events of the morning, she suddenly remembered Barry's boast. 'I have my successes, not quite so public, but lucrative.' Had he actually been alluding to his blackmail business? Rowena shuddered at his callousness. Maybe the women involved were 'spoilt little rich girls' but they did not deserve the misery Barry had put them through.

Rowena went wearily up to her office. Seeking out Clive's note, she dialled the number he had given her. When he answered she felt such relief flood through her at the sound of his voice that she found she was shaking. Her voice was husky as she fought back the tears of reaction.

'Rowena, are you all right?' Clive sounded irritable rather than concerned, as if he were annoyed she had rung him.

She drew a deep breath and said, 'Yes, I'm fine. It's just that we've had some trouble here this morning. I've dealt with it the best I can but I thought you ought to know exactly what's happened.'

She poured out the events of the morning, her voice growing stronger as her anger at Barry revived in the telling. Clive listened without interruption until she had finished, and then there was silence for a moment.

'Clive,' Rowena was anxious, 'are you there?'

'Yes,' came the abrupt reply. 'I'm thinking. The best thing to do is to swear Danny to secrecy on the extent of the matter but tell him to let it be generally known that Barry and Beryl were arrested for stealing. In Beryl's case it's true anyway, and in Barry's it's a partial truth. I'm afraid I have important engagements tonight and tomorrow, but I'll come down on Sunday evening and we'll decide exactly what to do then.'

'All right, I'll have a word with Danny. See you tomorrow evening.'

'It'll only be a flying visit,' Clive warned. 'I may be late, and I'll want to see Danny.'

Rowena felt a pang of disappointment. In her heart she had hoped Clive would suggest they had dinner together — she longed to spend just a little more time with him before the final break. But in her head she knew it was better that there should be no further intimacy between them.

'Fine,' she said, managing to keep her tone even, 'I'll be waiting in the bar.'

★   ★   ★

It was almost half-past ten when Clive finally walked into the bar the next evening. Rowena rose to greet him and suggested a drink.

He shook his head. 'No, let's go straight up to my office. Is Danny about?'

'Still in the kitchen, I think,' Rowena said. 'We can buzz him from the office.'

They went up and as Rowena called Danny on the house telephone, Clive picked up the mail on his desk and placed it, unopened, in his briefcase.

Danny came up at once and they all sat down to discuss the situation.

'It will all come out in court,' Clive said. 'I doubt if there's much we can do about that, but until then I suggest we stick to the story that stolen goods and money were found in Beryl's room and that Barry was implicated. As to the question of Mrs. Morton-Harvey's fur coat, we'll say it was taken in error and has now been returned to her.' Clive directed a straight look at Danny. 'I'd be extremely grateful if you continued to say nothing about the photographs, Danny,' he said. 'And I'm sure the ladies concerned would as well. It may seem a lot to ask, but consider for a moment how you would feel if it had been *your* wife.'

Danny, comparatively newly married and obviously devoted to his wife Linda, took the point and said he would say nothing not required of him by law.

When he had gone Clive and Rowena faced each other across the desk. She felt her heartbeat quicken as Clive looked at her. 'Now, this question of security. Obviously there is nothing the hotel can do about possible blackmail, but we must do something to ensure that petty thieving like Beryl's does not occur again.'

Rowena nodded her agreement, grateful that on this first occasion alone together since the dreadful moment on the terrace with Barry, Clive made no allusion to the incident and remained businesslike and aloof. Indeed if it weren't for the ferment of her own emotions, Rowena could see that her resignation, now safely in Clive's briefcase with his other mail, might not be necessary. But she knew in her heart that she must get away, for however businesslike their working relationship remained, her heart would be in torment as she strove to hide her love for him each and every day.

'How did Beryl have access to the bedrooms?' Clive asked.

'Pass key, I imagine,' Rowena replied. 'She was the waitress who usually dealt with room-service, and there would be occasions when she'd let herself in.'

'I see. Well, we'll have to try and work out some other system in future. Perhaps you'd like to call a meeting of the staff in the next few days. Much of what is needed can be done by implementing the ideas you outlined for me the other day. Just throw it open and see what reaction you get. Now as to Barry's commitments, you'll have to cancel any coaching arranged for the next two weeks, but after that I'll take over for the rest of this summer. It would be a pity to let the children's classes lapse so we'll certainly maintain those, and the adult lessons I'll fit in when I can.' Reading the surprise in Rowena's eyes he added coolly, 'I do coach, you know — the standard won't drop.'

Remembering how he had looked in practice Rowena had no fears in that direction, but she murmured that she didn't think he'd have the time to spare.

'Then I'll make it,' he replied. 'All young talent needs coaching and encouragement. It's most important the coaching should continue.'

When their discussion was over, Rowena got up to go. 'I'll say good night then, Clive.'

'I'm off again in the morning,' he said. 'And as seeing Short out of the cottage is no longer necessary, I won't come in on Friday. I'll have to see Kelland, but I think I'll go straight back to London then. You won't need me, will you?'

'No, I'll be fine. You haven't seen the

pool, of course, but it's coming along well.'

'Good. Set a provisional date for its grand opening and I'll see it when I pick you up on Friday week.'

'Friday week?'

Clive smiled for the first time since he had arrived that evening. 'I'm taking you to Wimbledon, remember? I'll pick you up at ten and we'll have lunch before play begins.'

Rowena opened her mouth to speak, to say that she was not sure yet that she could go, but Clive cut in smoothly: 'Wear something special, Ro. There's a cocktail party afterwards.'

She stared at him helplessly for an instant and then said softly, 'Good night, Clive.'

She was already halfway out of the door when she heard his answering, 'Good night.'

8

Wimbledon fortnight found her in a strangely confused frame of mind. Rowena's days were so busy that she felt in need of extra hours to get everything done, and yet, being days without Clive, they seemed to crawl by.

'This is what you've got to learn to live with,' she told herself sternly. 'Days without Clive are going to turn into life without Clive, so you'd better get used to the idea.'

She had not seen him again after that Sunday night for he had left very early. She was relieved for it had given him no chance to comment on her letter of resignation which he had picked up with the other letters on his desk.

She had decided to make no mention of it herself, for she felt that her letter would do the job far less emotionally than she could. But when on Monday morning she carried her post to her desk she found, lying to one side, the letter she'd addressed to Clive. In the turmoil of Saturday morning she had completely forgotten to place it on his desk. It was not, as she had thought, awaiting his attention in his briefcase, but still here among her other papers. She considered posting it on to him at once, but decided at last that the letter, though it was a necessary formality, was the coward's way out. She must tell him herself, face to face.

'I'll tell him after Wimbledon,' she thought feeling a little guilty at leaving it even later but unable to resist the temptation of one unspoiled day in Clive's company. 'After all,' she reminded herself, 'it's going to have to last a lifetime.'

The day dawned bright and clear, but showers and even thunderstorms were forecast. Having bathed and washed her hair, Rowena picked out one of the dresses she had chosen as possibilities for the day. It was delicate white crochet over a white silk underskirt, and its pretty scalloped neck-line and hem were trimmed with green. It also had a white lined jacket with three-quarter sleeves which she could wear if it grew chilly. Adding green shoes and hand-bag, Rowena surveyed herself critically in the mirror. She decided to leave her hair loose, sweeping her shoulders in a black silky curtain. Her make-up was delicately done, with only the faintest touch of blusher to bring colour to her pale cheeks. Her eyes, highlighted with soft green shadow, glowed in happy anticipation of the day she was determined to enjoy.

At exactly ten o'clock she went down to the hall and found Clive waiting for her. He smiled up at her as he saw her on the stairs and her heart missed a beat as his smile engulfed her, his eyes alight with pleasure as she approached him.

'I'm afraid I've got to pop in to David Kelland's office on the way,' he said as he settled her into the car, 'but it won't take long, and I've allowed enough time.'

Rowena remained in the car for the few moments Clive went in to see David Kelland and when he came back he tossed his briefcase on to the back seat and smiled across at her, his eyes creasing with delight.

'Right,' he announced. 'Wimbledon here we come.'

They cruised up the motorway and then skirted London, taking so many back ways that it was clear to Rowena that Clive had driven the route often.

There was little constraint between them as they discussed the progress of the pool conversion and then moved on to the tennis they were going to see.

★   ★   ★

At last, in an easy silence which had fallen between them, Rowena plucked up the courage to ask a question that had puzzled her.

'Clive,' she began tentatively.

'Mmm?'

'Clive, why were you and Donald estranged?'

'What?' He looked startled at the unexpected question.

'What was there between Donald and you? You clearly weren't very close, and even if the difference in your ages accounts for that, I've felt from him and then from you that there was something more.'

'Do you really want to know?'

'If you don't mind telling me,' she said, 'but not if you do.'

Clive smiled at that. 'I don't mind,' he said. 'You'll have to know soon anyway.'

'Why?' Rowena was surprised.

'It goes back a long way,' began Clive, ignoring her query. 'My father, Bill Latimer, married twice. First he married Donald's mother, Joan, and then after about twenty years, a young girl came into his office, a girl called Charlotte Blake. He fell in love with her, became completely and utterly

215

captivated by her. And so he left Donald's mother and moved in with Charlotte. Joan divorced him and after a while he and Charlotte got married.'

'And Charlotte's your mother?'

'Yes. Donald was in his early twenties by then and he was disgusted with his father. He never forgave him for leaving his mother; he never spoke to his father again, and so of course he had no contact with me when I came along. My father was much older than my mother and as time went on the marriage gradually disintegrated. When I was about thirteen my mother left my father and went off with someone else.'

'How awful!' cried Rowena. 'Did she take you?'

'No. I was really working at my tennis by then. I went to Millfield as a boarder and lived with my father in the holidays. He never really got over my mother leaving, and then he began to brood on how his first wife Joan must have felt. I think he tried to make contact with her but she wasn't interested, and Donald certainly didn't want to know.

'Anyway, he must have been feeling extremely guilty about it all because he made a new Will. In it he left everything to Donald. My father was a merchant banker, an extremely wealthy man, and I suppose he thought I'd be old enough to take care of myself when he died, and that he owed Donald something extra he didn't owe me. Who knows? I don't, there was no explanation in the Will. Anyway, he was killed in an air crash soon after I left school, and I found myself with almost nothing to live on.'

'What on earth did you do? He should have left you at least half his money.'

Clive grinned ruefully. 'That's what I thought at the time, but it all went to Donald who had to pay me a small monthly allowance while I was on the tournament circuit.'

'Surely he should have given you more?' Rowena was indignant. 'It would only have been common decency. You were his brother, after all.'

'I don't think he looked at it that way,' said Clive. 'He didn't want to think of me as a brother.'

'So what happened?'

'By then I was lucky enough to have found a sponsor and I began making some money on the circuit.'

'Did you ever meet Donald?' asked Rowena. 'You're so like him, to look at I mean.'

Clive smiled. 'Am I? I didn't really notice at the time. Yes, I met him once. He came to see me after the accident. You knew I'd been involved in a car crash?'

Rowena nodded. 'Yes, Barry told me.'

★ ★ ★

Clive gave a dry laugh. 'Yes, I expect he did. Well, after that, Donald visited me in hospital. At the time I already knew I'd never play serious tennis for a living again, but I wasn't sure if I'd even be

218

able to walk again.'

'Why did he come to see you then?'

Clive shrugged. 'At first I didn't know and I didn't care. My life seemed in ruins. I suppose Barry also told you my fiancée was killed in the crash?'

Rowena nodded again.

'Yes, I thought he wouldn't have missed that.'

'Clive,' Rowena looked at him sideways, 'did you know Barry before you came to Chalford Manor?'

Clive laughed. 'Oh, yes,' he said. 'I've known Barry from junior tournament days. He always was a bit of a Jack the lad.'

'I see,' said Rowena thoughtfully. 'Did you know he was employed at Chalford?'

'Not until I saw him there.'

'He sounded very bitter about you and your sports' shops.'

'He was always bitter,' remarked Clive. 'He never really made it in the tennis world and resented those of us who did. Anyway, with my career ruined, I was lucky enough to have Donald to help me pick up the pieces.'

'Donald did?' Rowena was incredulous. 'But I thought you said . . . '

'When he came to see me he offered to set me up in my own sports shop. Said he'd put up the capital from father's money and after that I'd be on my own.'

'And you made a go of it.'

'With a lot of help from my friends, yes, I did. I never met Donald again but a little while later he wrote to me and said since he was now unlikely to marry, and since his mother had died, he intended making me the sole beneficiary under his Will. But that was before you came into his life. Now, here we are.' Clive swung the car into the drive of a large house and parked it outside the garage. He got out and opened Rowena's door.

'But where are we?' asked Rowena as she got out.

'This is my house,' said Clive. 'It's just up the road from the All-England

Club. We'll leave the car here and walk down. I just want to put this indoors.' He opened his front door and put his briefcase inside while Rowena stood gazing up at the house. It was Tudor-style with a gable over the front door and a large stair window.

It must have at least five bedrooms, she thought inconsequentially, and the garden is beautifully kept.

★   ★   ★

Clive reappeared with a small badge pinned to his lapel. He handed a ticket to Rowena. 'You keep this,' he said. 'It gets you into the ground and into centre court. You'll have to show it each time you go in and out of the seats. Ready?' He grinned at Rowena's amazement and said, 'Let's go down.'

The hill was steep and Clive took Rowena's arm quite naturally as they walked down it. The warmth of his hand on her elbow was comforting.

Once inside the ground he bought

her a programme and then led her to the members' enclosure.

'Lunch?' he asked.

'But surely we can't go in there?'

'Why not?' grinned Clive. 'I'm a member, and you're my guest.'

'I don't believe all this,' thought Rowena allowing him to settle her at a small table shaded by a thatched umbrella. For a few moments he left her and she had a chance to look round at the people about her. One or two she recognised from the television and newspapers, but most were unfamiliar, all beautifully dressed, talking and laughing as they ate their lunch and drank their wine.

Clive reappeared with two large glasses. 'Hope you like Pimms,' he said, setting the drinks down on the table and disappearing again to return with two plates of cold chicken in a cream and curry sauce garnished with salad. 'I'll fetch the strawberries when we've finished this,' he said. 'Cheers.'

They ate their lunch in bright

sunshine but as they sat over coffee the sky darkened and within minutes there was the most tremendous thunderstorm. Everyone ran for cover with screams and laughter as the rain came down in stair-rods, the drops bouncing three foot from the ground. Clive and Rowena had taken shelter in the covered part of the enclosure as the clouds had gathered, but many people had not been quick enough and were drenched.

'Well, this wasn't meant to be part of the entertainment,' Clive laughed as he found her a seat well sheltered from the driving rain. The chandelier which hung from the centre of the awning shook ominously in the next roll of thunder and several people moved nervously from underneath it. The television monitors which normally showed play on both centre court and court number one seemed blank until Rowena peered at them more carefully and saw that what they were showing was a curtain of rain.

In the general hubbub Clive was greeted by several friends and as he introduced them to Rowena she found herself shaking hands with people whose names were familiar in the tennis world.

At last the storm slackened and they were able to go outside again. When the loudspeaker announced that play would commence shortly if there was no further rain, Clive led Rowena to their seats on centre court.

The rest of the day passed quickly, Rowena savouring every minute so as to remember it in the dark days ahead. The fact that she still had to tell Clive she was leaving was forced to the back of her mind. She'd face that when the time came; now she was determined nothing should spoil her day. The tennis they watched was very exciting, Curren battling with Connors to secure his place in a Wimbledon final, but even so Rowena found her eyes straying from the court to rest on Clive. He was unaware of her gaze, sitting hunched forward in his seat, completely enthralled in the game he was watching. This was how she would remember him, his face intent, his eyes aglow with excitement, the boy, the man, the tennis player all rolled into one.

9

At the end of the match they went and had tea and then returned to watch Jarryd and Becker fighting for the other place in the final. But the weather was not on their side and once more the heavens opened and play was abandoned for the day.

'That's a great pity,' Clive remarked as they left their scats. 'It's never the same match once there's been a break. The emphasis will all be different tomorrow.'

'Even so,' said Rowena, 'it's been a wonderful day.'

'It's not over yet,' declared Clive. 'We're going to the cocktail party now.' And for the third time he led her into the members' enclosure where they were plied with champagne and canapés as they moved among the throng of members and their guests in a hubbub of talk and laughter.

Clive knew a great many people and Rowena felt shy as he introduced her to his friends but they soon put her at ease even though several of them seemed to be eyeing her speculatively. One, an older man who had kept his glass filled from the start, said to her cheerfully, 'Glad Clive's found you. You look just what he needs.'

Rowena flushed with embarrassment and the man's wife said, 'Really George, behave,' and dragged him away.

At last the champagne stopped flowing and the guests drifted out into the dusk towards the gates. Rowena felt that perhaps she had had too much champagne. She knew Clive had had quite a lot and she wondered if she should offer to drive. He did not seem affected by the drink however and as they walked back up the hill in the twilight he again took her elbow to steady her progress on her high spiked heels.

When they reached the house, he said, 'Coffee I think, don't you?' and Rowena agreed.

'Sober you up a bit before you drive home,' she said.

'I'm not driving anywhere in this condition,' said Clive as he opened the front door and switched on the lights. 'Come in, Ro. I've got something to show you.'

She froze on the front doorstep.

'What do you mean?' she demanded. 'If you wanted me to drive you should have warned me before the party.'

'I don't want you to drive,' he snapped. 'For goodness' sake come in. It's beginning to rain again.'

Feeling the enormous drops of rain splashing down once more Rowena stepped inside and Clive closed the door behind her. Then he led her into a large sitting-room and said gruffly, 'Sit down, while I make some coffee.'

'But how are we going to get home?' she demanded.

'I am home,' he replied, 'and I don't

intend going out again tonight. We'll drive back to Chalford tomorrow. Don't worry, there are plenty of bedrooms. You can choose one to suit your mood or if you really want to you can call a cab to Paddington and take the train. Now sit still and relax while I make the coffee.'

★ ★ ★

Clive disappeared into the kitchen and Rowena flopped on to the sofa, fighting down her anger at the way she had been tricked into staying with him. He had known all along that he was not returning to Chalford Manor that night, and his deception had spoiled the end of a perfect day.

'I suppose that's a good thing,' she thought angrily. 'It won't be me who's spoilt the day when I tell him I'm leaving Chalford Manor. He's spoilt it already.' And she began to rehearse her resignation in her head.

Clive returned with the coffee. Seeing

Rowena sitting stiffly upright on the edge of her seat, he said placatingly, 'Look, Rowena, I'm sorry. I've had one accident because the driver had had too much to drink and as you know it altered my life. I don't plan to risk another. *Neither* of us is fit to drive.'

'The driver?' Rowena picked up sharply. 'Weren't you the driver?'

'No,' he said shortly. 'Caroline was driving.' He gave Rowena a long look and then enquired lightly, 'Barry?'

She nodded. 'Barry said you'd been driving and you'd killed your passenger.'

Clive gave a bitter laugh. 'Good old Barry,' he said. 'In with the boot wherever possible. He was determined to get you if he possibly could.'

'Barry was?' She looked incredulous.

'I saw the way he looked at you.'

Rowena gave a short laugh. 'He looked at every woman he met like that.'

'Perhaps,' Clive conceded and then calmly changed the subject and said, 'Coffee?'

She accepted the coffee, her mind whirling. Clive hadn't been responsible for anyone's death, nor the ruin of his own career. Fate had played him a cruel trick, and here she was angry that he was seeking to avoid a repetition.

'I'm sorry, Clive,' she said softly. 'I didn't realise, about your accident I mean. You're right. Neither of us should drive. But,' she added with some asperity, 'you might have warned me, I haven't even got a toothbrush!'

'Would you have come if I had?' asked Clive levelly.

Rowena hesitated. 'I don't know.'

'I wanted you to come,' he confessed. 'I've been planning this for weeks. I wanted to get you out of Chalford Manor, away from all its ghosts and memories, because I wanted us to talk.'

'What about?' she asked warily.

Clive reached over and took her coffee cup from her, and then sat down beside her, taking both her hands in his.

'Partly about Chalford,' he said, 'but from a distance.'

'About Chalford,' Rowena cut in. 'I wanted to say something, too. I'm sorry, Clive, but I've changed my mind. I'd like you to find another manager. I'm going to resign after all.' It came out abruptly, not at all as she had intended.

★ ★ ★

His grip on her hands tightened. 'Why?' he asked quietly.

She felt the colour creep into her cheeks and said shakily, 'I think it would be best. Easier for me to break away from the ghosts and memories like you said, and start something new.'

'And when did you come to this decision?' asked Clive coolly.

'I don't know. It just gradually crept up on me that this would be best all round.'

'After Barry Short made those stupid accusations at the Summer Ball, you mean,' said Clive, anger colouring his voice.

'How much did you hear?' she whispered, unable to look him in the face.

'Enough,' he said tightly.

'Then you must see it's better for both of us if I move on.' She tried to disengage her hands, but Clive would not release them. Instead he drew them in turn to his lips and placed a kiss in each palm.

Rowena drew in a sharp breath. 'Don't,' she muttered. 'Don't do that, Clive, please.'

'Why, Ro?' he replied, gently releasing one hand so that he could tilt her face to look at him. 'Why not?'

He saw the tears standing in her eyes and said huskily, 'Don't cry, my darling, don't cry. See, I'm not touching you now.' And he gently withdrew his hands. 'Ro, talk to me, tell me. There's something that frightens you. Help me understand.'

He spoke so softly and compassionately that suddenly Rowena began to explain, to tell him, as she had told no other man, what had happened to her on that long ago night and the way it had coloured her reactions to men ever since.

'I couldn't marry Donald knowing that I'd no real love to offer him.'

'Did he know?' Clive asked. 'Did you tell him this?'

'No,' she cried. 'I've never told anyone.'

'Except me,' he pointed out gently.

Rowena started. Finding that her hands had mysteriously returned to Clive's, she jerked them away and said despairingly, 'Barry was right. It was hateful of him to taunt me but it's true. I can't respond to anyone.'

'Rubbish,' said Clive vehemently. 'Utter vicious rubbish.'

'You don't know,' she wailed.

'Yes I do,' he answered firmly. 'You responded to me, remember? I held you in my arms and kissed you. And you kissed me, Ro. You put your arms round me and clung to me.'

'But only for a moment,' she

whispered, 'and then I panicked. I had to break free. Don't you see, I couldn't stand it?'

'Yes, I see,' said Clive. 'I see that you were afraid, perhaps of yourself as much as of me, but that's something we can overcome. Let me help you, Rowena. Please?'

Rowena looked at him in wonder. His eyes showed deep concern and more.

'Why?' she asked uncertainly.

'Because I love you, Ro.'

'What?' she stared unbelievingly at him.

'I love you. I've loved you from the moment you turned on me in that towering rage, the very first day I met you.' He grinned ruefully. 'I wouldn't admit it at first, even to myself, but believe me my darling, it's true. And ever since I've been scheming how to keep you near so I could teach you to love me, too.'

'But I can't,' she cried hopelessly. 'And you'll end up hating me.'

'Never. You're life to me, Rowena. All

that has happened up until now has brought me here, to you. All that has happened in your life has brought you here to me. I love you and I want you. I want to marry you, and father your children. You don't love me yet, you may never love me as much as I love you, but don't turn away.'

'I do love you, Clive.' Her voice was anguished. 'I love you more than I can believe. But don't you see, that's why I must turn away? I couldn't bear it if you ended up hating me, or worse still, repelled. I couldn't bear it if we married and then you turned to someone else for the part of love I wouldn't be able to give you.'

★ ★ ★

Her voice was unemotional now and its very flatness cried her despair to Clive.

'Tell me you love me,' he commanded.

'What's the point?'

'Just say it. If it's true, Ro, say it.'

236

'I love you, Clive.'

'And I love you; and now I'm going to kiss you, Rowena. I'm going to take you in my arms like this — ' and though her eyes grew wide in alarm he suited the action to the words — 'and I'm going to kiss you. If you feel frightened, say to yourself, 'This is Clive kissing me, because he loves me.' And if you are still frightened just pull free. I promise you I'll let you go at once.'

Rowena felt his arms, sure and strong about her, and his warm breath on her cheek as he lowered his head to touch her lips with his in a brief butterfly kiss. She closed her eyes as he began to kiss the rest of her face, tiny kisses upon her forehead, eyes and nose, her cheeks and chin and hair. Then, as she did not pull away, his lips returned to hers and very softly and gently began to kiss her with controlled passion. Of their own volition her arms slid around his neck and drew him closer.

237

For a moment he held her cradled against him, rocking her gently like a frightened child. Then he kissed her again and her lips parted in return. For a second the familiar panic crept into her body and she stiffened.

Immediately Clive released her, and murmured reassuringly, 'It's all right, my darling. It's Clive, and I adore you, Rowena.'

She looked up into his face, his strong handsome face, and saw that what he said was true. A fierce fire burned in his eyes, but his expression was one of such tenderness that she buried her face against him in awe that such love should be given unasked to her. Again he held her gently, until she raised her face shyly to his. Then, with a groan, he began to kiss her again.

★   ★   ★

Rowena found herself clinging to him, returning kiss for kiss, while the most unfamiliar sensations flooded her entire body. When at last he let her go she was trembling, her heart was hammering, and she felt as weak as a baby.

'You see, my love,' Clive whispered, his lips against her ear, 'there's nothing to be afraid of. Let me love you,' he murmured as he felt her response. 'Let me be the first and last man to love you, Rowena.'

Rowena's eyes met his in mute appeal and as she raised her arms to him, Clive gathered her up as if she weighed no more than thistledown and strode upstairs to his bedroom.

Drowning in the unexpected response of her own body, Rowena clung to him and felt his need of her. Then, even as she wondered at the feel of him against her, his body firm against her own softness, Clive gently let her go so that no part of him touched her. The sensation of loss was overwhelming. Rowena turned to look at him.

'Clive?' Her voice was husky with desire.

'Mmm,' he murmured, almost sleepily.

'Don't leave me.'

'I'm here. Don't be afraid.'

'I'm not afraid, Clive. I love you.' She reached out a trembling hand and touched his chest. 'Please make love to me, Clive, I need you.'

His eyes bored into hers and it seemed suddenly that he was the vulnerable one and she the strong.

'Say that again,' he demanded huskily. 'Tell me again.'

Rowena spoke with deliberate care. 'I love you, I need you and I want you, Clive.' She might have said more, but the opportunity was denied her as, with a groan, Clive pulled her down beneath him and closed her mouth with his own.

All Rowena's fears were banished, all constraint between them gone, and Clive drew her on to greater heights of pleasure and intoxication, claiming her mind and body.

* * *

At last, lying quiescent beside him, Rowena heard Clive say gruffly: 'Don't you ever dare try to tell me you're frigid again, Miss Winston. It would be a lie.'

Rowena laughed softly. Turning her face to his, she kissed him gently.

'But only with you,' she murmured.

'So I should hope,' he replied. 'Only with me, always with me. Promise?'

'Promise.'

Clive kissed her again at that. Then, suddenly breaking free, he said, 'Wait here a moment.' He shrugged on a silk dressing-gown and left the bedroom. He was back almost at once with his briefcase.

'Here,' he said, extracting a sheaf of documents and handing them to her.

Intrigued Rowena took the papers and looked at them. After a moment's stunned silence she looked up at Clive who stood at the end of the bed watching her quizzically.

'What's all this?' she whispered.

'It's Chalford,' he replied easily. 'You see, I've had it made over to you.'

'You've what?' she shrieked.

'I know now that Donald really meant you to have the place. He simply forgot to sign the Will. You belong there, and once probate has been granted it'll be yours.'

'Oh, Clive,' she cried. 'You can't! I can't!'

'Why not? Morally the place is yours. I don't need it or want it. I have my own business concerns, you know that. Let's do what Donald wanted. It's yours, Ro. David Kelland's drawn up all the necessary papers — and I *have* signed them.'

'Clive, it's not because . . . ' began Rowena thinking of the terrible conversation between herself and Barry which he had overheard.

'It's not because of anything,' Clive interrupted firmly, 'except that it was what Donald intended.'

'But you said . . . ' Rowena tried again, and again Clive interrupted.

'I said a great many stupid and ill-conceived things when I first met you,' he agreed, 'all of which I have since regretted!' Seeing she was unconvinced he sat down beside her on the bed once more and said, 'If it makes you any happier, it can be your wedding present.'

'Wedding present?' Rowena looked startled.

'My darling heart, haven't you just this moment promised you'll never practise your newly acquired skills on anyone but me?'

In wonder, Rowena could only nod.

'Then I think we'd better get married, don't you? Please?' he added almost as an afterthought. As Rowena nodded again, still not trusting herself to speak, Clive began to kiss her.

David Kelland's carefully prepared documents slid to the floor unheeded as Rowena melted into Clive's arms.

'You see,' he murmured encouragingly, 'you improve every minute.' His love for her glowed in his eyes.

'Perhaps it's because I've so much time to make up.'

'Then we'd better not waste a minute more,' Clive said firmly. 'Had we?'

And she could only agree.

THE END

We do hope that you have enjoyed reading this large print book.

Did you know that all of our titles are available for purchase?

We publish a wide range of high quality large print books including:
Romances, Mysteries, Classics
General Fiction
Non Fiction and Westerns

Special interest titles available in large print are:
The Little Oxford Dictionary
Music Book, Song Book
Hymn Book, Service Book

Also available from us courtesy of Oxford University Press:
Young Readers' Dictionary
(large print edition)
Young Readers' Thesaurus
(large print edition)

For further information or a free brochure, please contact us at:
Ulverscroft Large Print Books Ltd.,
The Green, Bradgate Road, Anstey,
Leicester, LE7 7FU, England.
Tel: (00 44) **0116 236 4325**
Fax: (00 44) **0116 234 0205**

FOREVER IN MY HEART

Joyce Johnson

With the support of a loving family, Julie Haywood is coping well with the trauma of divorce and the difficulties of single parenthood. Well on track with her medical career, she is looking forward to an exciting new promotion — not realising it will bring her into contact with Rob, a part of her past she has tried to forget. Then, when ex-husband Geoff turns up, Julie finds she has some hard decisions to make . . .

THE SKELTON GIRL

Gillian Kaye

1812: These are tempestuous times in the wool mills of the Pennine moors. Randolf Staines is introducing new machinery to Keld Mill, which will put many of the villagers out of work. Diana Skelton, whose father used to own Keld Mill, takes a strong dislike to Randolf, and when there is trouble amongst the dismissed croppers she becomes involved. It is only after a night of violence at the mill that Diana and Randolf begin to see eye to eye . . .

A NEW LIFE FOR ROSEMARY

Anne Holman

Alone since the loss of her family in an air-raid, Rosemary — newly demobbed from the WRNS — returns to her old home. But she is shocked to find that a whole family has been temporarily housed there . . . With little knowledge of children and cooking, and with housework to do, she has her hands full — especially when strange things begin happening at the bottom of her garden . . . Friends help her cope, as she helps them. But will she also cope when romance calls?

A CHANGE OF HEART

Karen Abbott

Abigail Norton's dream of owning her own beauty salon seems to be coming true when she finds the ideal location in a Merseyside village. But someone is determined to thwart her plans . . . Abbie can't help wondering if Tim Boardman, handsome owner of the travel agent premises next door, is trying to wreck her dream in order to expand his own property. When things take a more sinister turn, she wonders to whom she can turn for help . . .

THE FERNHURST INHERITANCE

Mary Cummins

Laura and Robert Faulkner are drifting apart — and is it any wonder, when Robert spends every available moment working? It doesn't help that he is attracted to his business partner, the worldly, glamorous Stella . . . Meanwhile, their son Neil Faulkner, back from a year in America, finds himself falling in love with their houseguest, Susan. Susan, however, has worries of her own to contend with . . .